The Other Side of the Family

MAUREEN POPLE

Borzoi Sprinters · Alfred A. Knopf
NEW YORK

DR. M. JERRY WEISS, Distinguished Service Professor of Communications at Jersey City State College, is the educational consultant for Borzoi Sprinters. A past chair of the International Reading Association President's Advisory Committee on Intellectual Freedom, he travels frequently to give workshops on the use of trade books in schools.

A BORZOI SPRINTER PUBLISHED BY ALFRED A. KNOPF, INC.
Copyright © 1986 by Maureen Pople
Cover art copyright © 1990 by Kenneth Spengler
All rights reserved under International and Pan-American Copyright Conventions. Published in the United States by Alfred A. Knopf, Inc., New York. Distributed by Random House, Inc., New York. Hardcover edition published in the United States in 1988 by Henry Holt and Company, Inc. Originally published in Australia in 1986 by University of Queensland Press. Published by arrangement with Henry Holt and Company, Inc.

Library of Congress Catalog Card Number: 87-32929
ISBN: 0-394-83854-8
RL: 5.2

First Borzoi Sprinter edition: March 1990
Manufactured in the United States of America
1   2   3   4   5   6   7   8   9   10

For my daughters
Alison and Bridget

1

They were talking about me again. I knew it the moment my hand touched the doorknob. So of course I stepped back to listen.

"She can't stay here any longer, George."

"Harbor full of Jap submarines and not a single pin to my name."

"I *am* sorry for the poor child."

I was sorry for her too, standing in the drafty hallway, trying to make sense of what they were saying. They had a habit of moving a lot as they talked and another one of not listening to a solitary thing that was said to them. They were doing both now. I could hear my grandfather crashing about among the furniture, opening drawers and banging cupboard doors. Grandmother was setting the table for breakfast, her voice fading as she went into the kitchen and growing louder as she came back and started throwing plates and jars of jams and packets of cereal at the table. Not in anger. She always does it, to show the world and Grandpa in particular that she is not yet accustomed to living in a small flat and doing all the housework herself.

"Coming all this way on that terrible ship. For a child her age what a life she's had." *Rattle splat*.

"Pins, Margaret!" *Dong, boing*. "Pins!"

So they beat their way about, filling the room with movement while their conversational paths seldom met.

"She'll just have to go soon."

"Major attack, woman. How do I cope without my box of pins?"

"Indigestion!" Grandmother shouted from the kitchen. The popping noises she always made when she lit the gas stove reminded me of gunfire and made me nervous. I could feel my hands and forehead go clammy, a promise of pimples to come. And was she suggesting that Grandfather Dawson had eaten the pins? Having won the morning's battle with the gas she came back into the living room, leaving the vanquished stove to hiss sullenly in the kitchen.

"Indigestion! You had it right after Pearl Harbor. No, I tell a lie, it was the Coral Sea Battle and you needed extra colors for the American fleet."

Ah, *those* pins! I understood now what all the fuss was about; obviously he'd swallowed the stupid things. About three weeks ago, and they'd given him indigestion. Fair enough, it served him right.

"You think . . . bathroom cabinet . . . The bathroom cabinet?" They spoke at the same time. Together at last!

I grabbed the door and opened it wide before Grandfather could come bashing through and find me there.

"Good morning," I said, and they looked at me as if for a moment they'd forgotten completely who I was. It didn't bother me, I was getting used to it.

The blackout curtains had been pulled back, Grandfather's first task every morning. He had to check to see that no one had stolen his precious harbor during the night. No one had, God was in his heaven, all was right with the world. It still filled the window as if a vast cinema screen had been pasted there. I looked for the Japanese Navy but there were in view only three small naval vessels covered in dreary camouflage paint. A tram jerked and twitched its way around Bennelong Point, and a Manly ferry was starting off from Circular Quay. Not a submarine in sight. No doubt they'd dived for the bottom when they heard the Dawson grandfolks shouting.

"Did you sleep well?" I asked. But Grandfather was out the door and Grandmother, looking embarrassed—and so she should after what she'd said about me—was heading for the kitchen again. I wondered, not for the first time since I'd come to live with them, if it would be any use at all to scream, or bang my head against the wall, or jump up and down a lot. While I thought about it I wandered across and straightened up the pile of china, cutlery and food that Grandmother had dumped on the table.

She came back, her face in order again. "Big day for your grandfather, dear," she said. "Japanese submarines in the harbor, they say." She made it sound as if they were conducting the war just to amuse Grandfather, and I exploded.

"Grandmother! There's a war on! How can he enjoy it so much? And all this! I mean, it's—it's bizarre!"

Then shame punched me in the stomach and I felt rotten. "Well, I mean, it's . . ."

"No, no." She beamed, proud of my dexterity with the English language, "Bizarre is good. Yes, that map is bizarre, I'll admit. *Bizarre*."

"But it's also very . . . impressive."

"Well, yes, it is. And so very interesting for your grandfather."

And only for him! There could not be a single person in the whole world apart from Grandfather Dawson who would be remotely interested in the vast map that covered the entire side wall of the room. When I first arrived in Sydney it made me realize as nothing else had that I had indeed journeyed to the Antipodes. Instead of Great Britain being in the center as it should be, neatly balanced by Europe and Asia on one side and by America, North and South, on the other, here it was cramped up in a remote corner. The main part was taken up by a great expanse of ocean, with Australia and New Zealand stuck in the middle of it, hogging center stage like actors new to the craft. And the whole thing just bristled with colored pins. Bunches of bright red in the ocean.

"Ships of the Australian Navy," Grandfather explained to me. "Should be blue, I suppose, being the Navy, but then they wouldn't show up very well on the map would they? Being at sea, you understand. So I've made the RAAF blue, and the brown, that's the AIF, closest to khaki I could find in the shop."

In the tiny region of the map that was Europe a few small clusters of the least popular colors were scattered, pinks, purple, and a washy lime-green. Thanks to the Australian Navy, poor old England, which as everyone knows is always red on the map, had to make do with a palish pink. There was a lot of black in the Pacific, the good old US of A, a good strong color for them. It made me feverish to hear Grandfather talk about our gallant allies, saving our skin and all the rest of it. I'd heard my mother on the United States, and believe me she didn't think much of them for not coming into the

4

war sooner, when Britain could have done with a bit of help.

Now Grandfather was back, clutching his pins. They were kept in a round box with *Collars* written across the top in curly gold lettering. He groped gingerly and came up with five yellow ones which he plunged viciously right into the center of Sydney Harbour. Then, sucking his pinholed fingers: "Just across from where you were sleeping, my girl. Five at least of the murderous beggars. Probably more. Terrible row they made."

I hadn't heard a thing, although I had dreamed of London and a bombing raid, but then I often did.

"Saw the whole show myself," he boasted. Pity it hadn't been his night for being air raid warden, he'd have had a great time then. "Lots of rumors going about of course, but we'll see what comes over on the next bulletin." Grandpa really would have enjoyed the Blitz!

"Why don't you pop down to the bowling club, George dear? After breakfast. See what you can find out." Grandmother could foresee a long day's vigil by the wireless, an enormous walnut console which, as usual, was crackling quietly away in its corner, waiting for the volume to be turned up to a deafening pitch when news time came around again.

"Bowling club? What on earth could I possibly learn there? Those fellows don't keep the check on this war that I do. You know that, Margaret."

"Oh, I doubt if anyone in the whole country does that, dear," and good old Grandmother didn't smile as she said it. Not the slightest twitch.

After breakfast he did set out for the bowling club, wearing his red blazer with the embroidered pocket and his white hat with the crest on the front, carrying his walking stick and the morning paper.

"Don't you hurry back now, dear," Grandmother called from the side window as he came out the door of the building. Then she turned to me and I hoped she might tell me what she'd been trying to talk to Grandpa about earlier, and why I had to leave. Then I hoped even harder that she wouldn't. Because, although living with the Dawsons was ghastly compared to being at home in London with my mother and father, there was absolutely nowhere else I could possibly go.

Or so I thought.

2

I set off for school at the usual time, and hurried up the hill to the tram stop. I always hurried in case Grandmother was watching through the side window. Then I let two trams go by and caught the third. I always did this too, because the maneuver guaranteed that I would arrive at school about the same time as the bell rang. Sure enough, as I crept through the gate it clanged and my fellow pupils came pounding across the asphalt from all directions, like herds of stampeding wildebeests, to line up for Assembly. The headmaster and two teachers stood on the landing at the top of the main steps and at least one of them had something to say to the school each day. No one ever listened.

My class, 3A, was toward the back, so I slunk around and joined the end of the girls' line. I put my case between my feet and clenched my ankles firmly against it, because someone had nicked it during my first week at school. It was found eventually, intact, but in the boys' lavatory and I'd made myself a promise not to let it out of my sight again. The thought that some oafish boy might have looked inside it still made my ears smolder.

The animals were more restless than usual today and I had to put up with pestering remarks.

"How ja do? So kaind of yew to come."

"One does deplore these rough colonials, doesn't one?"

"One certainly does," I hissed and regretted with the same breath as I felt my school case bounce, kicked from the row behind. I turned, to find the acned face of the class wit about three inches from my own. Acned face.

He crossed his eyes and growled, "Hey, cobber, how ya doin', eh?"

I'd been three months with this lot and I disliked them all just as much as I had the day I arrived. Every single one of them, and specially those boys.

At the beginning they were at least interested in me because I was new. The fact that I'd come out from England gave me some extra curiosity value and they used to cluster around at recess and question me about the bombings. The girls, that is. But after about a week interest waned and they all went back in to their own tight little groups. Some of them were pleasant enough without being at all friendly and some were downright rude, like the ones teasing me today. The boys didn't notice me at all. It seems to be a convention in Australia that boys and girls are never to be seen talking together in a mixed group, and so at school they gather in herds at the farthest ends of the grounds and although they do a lot of looking at each other, they never speak. Goodness knows how they act at parties. I've never been invited to one.

But today, *mirabile dictu*, there was a sisterly gesture from one of the other girls. Linda Craig was farther up the row and she slid down between the lines and nudged in beside me. The headmaster was still droning on quite contentedly. Linda snarled at the cross-eyed one, "Why don't you leave her alone, Pea-brain?" and he immediately returned his eyeballs to their regular position and crooned, "Ah, the lovely Linda. Darlin' *je vous aime beaucoup*." This sent his row of followers into stitches again.

She ignored him and asked if I wanted to eat lunch with her. I longed for the courage to say no thanks, I have another engagement, but of course I had neither an engagement nor that lion kind of courage, and anyway I wanted to very much. So I nodded to indicate the minimum of enthusiasm and we turned with the others and shuffled across to the steps and into school.

Recess was still a problem. She'd said "lunch" and I didn't want to try my luck too far. I wasn't bothered anyway. Recess, being only about twenty minutes long, was easily managed. I took a large notebook and my fountain pen and with an expression of earnest preoccupation bustled past the rest of the class as they milled around the doorway. There was then the passageway to be dealt with. I paused for a moment at the largest of the notice boards that lined its walls and carefully scrutinized the latest list that had been thumbtacked to it. Horrors! I'd chosen to study the list of boys chosen to play for the school in some football match! But it gave anyone who wanted to ask me to sit with them during recess the chance to do it. Nobody did, so I hurried up the stairs to the library.

Miss Carpenter was the librarian and as usual she was touchingly glad to see me. No one ever visited the library of their own free will except me and it must have been a joy to her to see a visitor who wasn't being towed in by a teacher. As usual I chose the table by the window and she sat in her little cubbyhole of a desk and stared

9

at me with a mixture of triumph and adoration. A prize. A reader. Again as usual I chose a book with pictures of England and sat there in the wintry sunshine poring over the illustrations and luxuriating in homesickness. To think and think about something wonderful, like being home again, and seeing Mummy and Dad and my friends, and being just on the edge of crying, but managing not to, is to me an almost enjoyable emotion. A worthwhile experience in a peculiar sort of way. Like being a Stoic. I test myself like that sometimes. This day it was harder than usual to keep from putting my head down onto the gouged and ink-stained wood and bawling like a baby.

It had not been a very good year for me. Nor had the year before, come to that, or the year before that, but at least then I'd been at home with my parents.

It was when my father enlisted that things began to fall apart for me. Until then the war seemed a problem that was someone else's job to solve. Then one evening my parents sat down with me and told me that he was going into the air force and wasn't it splendid that they'd agreed to take him. I didn't think it splendid at all and I howled and howled until he carried me into my room and tossed me on the bed and ordered me to stop because my crying was hurting Mother. She was upset. I really did feel that I had a right to be upset too, but I stopped crying, at least until the lights were out and I could shove my head under the pillow. Soon after that my mother went to work in the office of the hospital around the corner and the rotten Germans started to bomb London.

It would have been all right if the news hadn't got out to Australia, but as soon as the Dawson grandparents (my mother's family) heard about the bombing they started their campaign and before I knew what they were plotting, and without being consulted at all, I found myself on an enormous great ship being transported to the colonies like a convict! Although we were in a convoy of ships that were supposed to guard us, all of us children were scared out of our wits most of the time. The grown-ups on board did try to keep us amused and were wonderfully kind but they weren't very good at lip buttoning, and they swapped stories of torpedoes and magnetic mines just about all of the time. All in all it was a voyage I'd be happy to forget, and at the end of it I knew I had to meet and live with a pair of Australian grandparents I'd never seen. And be pleasant and polite, helpful, and all the things that my mother kept thinking of and reminding me about as the time came near to leave her. I didn't think it was at all fair, specially as all my friends at school were staying on and were most sympathetic about my having to go.

While I'm at it I may as well finish off my list of grievances, I suppose. When we arrived in Sydney I was an awful mess. All twitches from some fright we had during the trip, which took almost three months instead of six weeks. We set off from Liverpool and there were some terrible gales in the North Atlantic, so as well as the danger from German submarines and planes there was the chance of colliding with the other ships in the convoy as we all wallowed about. Sometimes we lost sight of the other ships altogether and that was even more scary than the fear of colliding. We went all the way to Rio de Janeiro to pick up some cargo, then across to Cape Town. Most of the people got off there, lucky ducks, they missed the Indian Ocean, where, you can take my word for it, the seas can be very rough indeed. So there was seasickness to add to my woes and the

11

worst part of that is that God won't let you die when you want to, even when you plead with him and promise anything! Believe me, being hit by a bomb or a torpedo wouldn't have upset me as much as not dying from seasickness did. There was also the dread of meeting the relatives and having to leave the other children I'd got to know on the ship. There were twenty-four altogether, five of them about my age, and we all promised to keep in touch, although none of the others has answered my letters yet. We also made a vow to meet by one of the lions in Trafalgar Square at noon on September 3 every year to see how we're all getting on, and if any of us need any help the others have all promised to see what they can do. That is if we ever get back to England!

When we finally arrived in Sydney I was in no mood to admire the harbor that my parents had told me so much about, it was just another harbor to me, only bigger than most. The ship berthed at a place called Pyrmont and to get there we had to go right under the Harbour Bridge, which seemed dangerously low, but the ship scraped under it without losing anything.

The Dawsons were at the wharf to meet me and as soon as my grandmother set eyes on me she started to cry and I swear she didn't stop for about five days. Maybe it was because she was disappointed when she finally got to see me—I do have very fat lips—although she swore at the time that it was because I reminded her of her darling Anne. (That's my mother, in whom there is not the slightest glint of similarity to me!)

They took me home in a taxi. Not a bit like the London ones, just an ordinary car really, but with a big black gas bag on top, and Grandfather and the driver talked about the petrol shortage and rationing all the way home just as if I hadn't come all this way by myself.

12

Grandmother, of course, cried. They live at Kirribilli, which is on the harbor. To get there we had to cross the bridge, so that was twice in one day I'd been in contact with it. Grandfather interrupted his petrol saga to tell me that he'd been there when the bridge was opened and a man named de Groot rode up on a horse and cut the ribbon with his sword before the premier was able to do it. It was a fairly dull story the way he told it, and he didn't explain what a Dutchman was doing there riding about on a horse anyway. I didn't ask.

Things were livened up a bit when we arrived at the block of flats where they live. The other five families who live there had hung a huge Union Jack above the front entrance and a banner saying *Welcome, Kate*, which I thought was rather sweet. They also put on a yummy meal which they called afternoon tea; it was more like a banquet actually. I couldn't remember seeing so much food for ages. Someone put Grandmother to bed, still sobbing, and they all hung about exclaiming over me until I dropped off to sleep myself, right there at the dining table!

And now, it seemed, my grandparents, who had been so frantic to have me stay with them, wanted me to go.

Fortunately the bell to end recess pulled things together for me and I dashed back to the classroom, putting my book on Miss Carpenter's desk as I passed. She liked us to do that, I think, because it gave her something to occupy her time. She was always giving yawny little talks on the joys of the Dewey decimal system, but nobody paid any attention. Poor Miss Carpenter, I don't think she had a boyfriend and she was too old by far to enlist in something and get away from the school and all those book haters.

3

We had Latin and history periods after recess and I'm quite good at both of those so the time passed quickly. When the bell rang for lunch I took my parcel of sandwiches from my case and stayed at my desk as long as I could to let the rest of them go out. I decided that I'd walk behind Linda, so that if she remembered about my eating with her she could turn around and look for me, and if she didn't I'd be able to detour libraryward again. So I loitered along the corridor, ready to peruse another of the boring lists on the wall if she turned and didn't take any notice of me. It was slow progress. Every time the crowd she was with paused I had to as well, because I would have died if I'd caught up with them and they'd looked at me as if I shouldn't have been there. Mercifully as they arrived at the outer doorway she turned and yelled at me, "You coming? Farthest tree!" and she and two of the other girls set off at a brisk jog across the school yard. I followed and caught up with them just as they settled in on the seats at the base of a scruffy old palm tree. We all spread our belongings about so that no one could join who hadn't been invited and Linda took charge of the conversation straight away.

"Hey," she said. "You don't want to take any notice of those dopes in lines. They only tease you because you bite back every time. They're all dopes anyway, except Mike Thomas. He's OK."

"OK? Mike Thomas? That cross-eyed idiot?"

Three indignant faces turned on me.

"He only crosses them in fun. He *surfs*."

"He's a champion swimmer but. Bronze medal!"

"He just happens to be a lifesaver, that's all!"

Marvelous, isn't it? He can be as rude as he likes and as uncouth as anyone could ever imagine, but if he's half decent at any kind of sport at all, *then* he's a fine person!

"Marvelous," I said, really trying not to sound sarcastic. "I didn't know he was a life . . . what is a lifesaver exactly?"

They reminded me I'd claimed my father was an Australian, so how come I didn't know about lifesavers, huh?

"He is too, but he went to England sixteen years ago, and I don't know if he knows about . . . well of course he would, I suppose the subject just never came up." And why am I being so apologetic, for heaven's sake? Why should the whole world know about your stupid old lifesavers? Or care. I don't, not really. Only asked to be pleasant since it seems so important to you. And I still can't tolerate Mike Thomas, lifesaver or not, so there.

It's comforting to be able to think things privately while your face looks as if you're not thinking at all. I do it rather well, and often. They, unaware of my thoughts, were delighted to have such an ignoramus in

15

their midst, so I could hardly blame them for offering me an interminable explanation of the skills of the lifesaver.

"They patrol the beaches in summer. They put flags on the beach first to show you where the rips and that are and you've got to bathe between the flags, and they have a sort of tower on the beach and they sit up there and watch . . ."

"He dashes out with the line around his waist and they reel you in."

". . . artificial respiration till you're breathing."

"Or bung you off to hospital in the ambulance."

"Unless you're taken by a shark . . ."

"I don't think I'll bother with the beach."

"Oh, Kate! Everybody goes to the beach in summer!"

"If only to watch the lifesavers!" And they all fell about giggling and I wondered if it would be worth the bother of trying to be friends with them. I decided that it probably would.

But beaches were out now, war was in.

"Hey, what about last night then, eh? My dad heard there were Jap subs in the harbor. Anybody hear anything?"

They all had of course. I was the only one who'd slept through it. Judy had a brother who had a friend whose father had actually been on the Manly ferry at the time, so she knew all about it. Depth charges, torpedo explosions, shrapnel from bursting shells falling like hail, searchlights making the whole harbor as bright as daylight, navy vessels dashing about at top speed, Verey lights, pom-pom guns, tracer bullets! Truly a ferry ride to remember for the rest of your life.

According to Linda, her grandfather had organized the defenses of the city practically single-handed. He'd been on air raid warden duties and had to dash up thousands of stairs to warn people that their lights were showing and then he had an altercation with a taxi driver which I wish I'd been there to see. The taxis have blackout shades fitted to their headlamps, but when they go over a bump the light shows upward and any enemy aircraft that might happen to be passing at the time can see that there's a taxi down there below. So Linda's grandfather stopped this taxi and told the driver to go more slowly, or adjust his shades or something and the driver got out and offered to punch him, but Linda's grandfather was wearing his tin hat and his spectacles so the driver decided not to bother. I think my Grandpa Dawson and Linda's grandfather could become firm friends if they should ever meet.

Cathy claimed to have been awake all night, hysterical with fear, but Linda soon cut her off.

"My mum says we'll be bombed next. What's it like being bombed?"

So I realized why she'd invited me to sit with them, as an authority on bombings. Still, anything was better than eating alone with a book propped on your knee.

"Yes, I've been in air raids," I said.

"The Blitz? Like right in London?"

"Oh yes." I try to sound offhand when I talk about it, but it's hard to be blasé about those terrifying nights. "We lived in a part called Bloomsbury and every night for ages we had to go down into the Underground because of the raids."

"Underground? You mean tunnels? Wow!"

"She means air-raid shelters, you dill. Split trenches."

"Slit trenches. But these were railway stations actually. It was pretty awful, but fun sometimes. We used to take our supper and blankets down and everyone

17

was cheerful. They were all sort of kind to one another and in the morning when you went up again, you'd see the smoke and the buildings that'd been hit . . ."

"I thought they evacuated the children to the country."—From Cathy, who'd recovered from her night of hysteria and was looking for an argument.

"Yes, they did. For a while they sent me to a town in Somerset, Burnham-on-Sea . . ."

"Oh, well then."

I went on quickly. "But that wasn't far from Bristol and the Germans bombed there too. Aircraft factories, you know."

"Hey, listen. We wouldn't have enough underground stations! I mean, we'd all have to go into the city to find a shelter."

"They're building a huge one under the Queen Victoria Building."

"Gee, great. Hey, Kate, did they partition you off or anything? I mean, did you all sleep down there? Hey, we might meet some boys that way."

"Oh, Cathy! Shut up, will you? What about your parents then? They still over there?"

"My mother works in a hospital and Dad's in the air force."

"Ooh! A Spitfire pilot?"

"Hey, was he one of the First of the Few?"

"What's he fly?"

But suddenly I'd had enough of the war. "I'm sorry," I said, "I'd rather not talk about it if you don't mind."

"Sure, kid." Linda patted my arm. "My dad's in the RAAF, guess he'll be going away soon. He's a rear gunner but. Your father in bombers?"

The merciful bell rang and my bacon was saved. I scrabbled in the dirt to retrieve the linen table napkin

Grandmother Dawson insisted I bring with my lunch each day, we all dashed to the bins with our garbage, then back into class again.

That afternoon I didn't linger about the schoolroom until the others had all gone, but joined them in the rush toward the tram shelter and climbed on board with Cathy when my tram finally trundled up. Cathy was tall and gawky and talked a lot, but it was a help that day because I'd begun to dread arriving home in case the Dawsons had already put my suitcase outside the door.

"My sister, she works in a bank and she's met this Yank, see. He's gorgeous! Nine feet tall, crew-cut hair and the most deevine drawly voice. 'Hi, you-all,' he says, and Mum and me we just die! He's got this friend, see, his buddy, and Mum says I can go to the pictures with them one night."

I began to count the stops.

"If it works out I'll get you a date too. You interested?"

"I don't think my grandparents would let me, but thanks anyway." Let me! They'd instantly faint dead away at my feet if I as much as suggested a date with a serviceman. If I said he was American they'd pass away on the spot.

"Oh well, I'll let you know how it goes and you could try asking them. His name's Dwayne, my sister's bloke. Dwayne. Chocolates, nylons . . ."

"Here's my stop."

"Hooroo, then. Hey, you must have a great view of the harbor. Lovely innit?"

"Oh yes, it must be the most beautiful harbor in the world, I think." And I slunk off the tram like the craven creature that I was.

4

As I walked down the hill I caught glimpses of the water between the buildings. Still no sign of Grandfather's submarines and nothing much had changed since morning. The naval vessels still floated drably in their corner, two small ferries were passing near the quay, a tram was rounding Bennelong Point and trains, trams and cars were thundering across the Harbour Bridge.

I untied my key from the corner of my handkerchief and let myself into the flat. And had the impression immediately that they'd been talking about me again. They sat at the table drinking tea and nibbling at Sao biscuits with cheese toasted on top. Grandfather was carrying out an audit on his colored pins and Grandmother looked nervous. But, ever polite, she gave me the usual greeting. "Well, dear, how did it go at school today?"

And I gave her my usual reply. "Quite well, thank you, Gran. And how was your day?"

But she didn't follow our customary routine. Instead she said, "Sit down, dear. Your grandfather and I have something to say to you."

She looked so solemn that I immediately thought the very worst had happened and a great heavy boulder fell from somewhere and thudded into the center of my chest. But it wasn't bad news from England after all.

"There's been an official announcement . . ."

"A communiqué . . ."

"Three Japanese . . ."

"From Allied Headquarters, Melbourne . . ."

"Oh, very well, George. You tell her." She must have been really upset to give in so quickly.

So Grandfather told me about the announcement from the headquarters of the Allied Commander in Chief, General Douglas MacArthur. Using every official term and every piece of war jargon he could muster. There'd been three Japanese midget submarines in the harbor the night before. One of their torpedoes didn't explode, but another hit an old ferry that was being used as a naval depot ship. Ten men were injured, eight were killed and eleven were still missing. He stood up very straight and still as he told me and spoke in a trembly voice. I felt suddenly limp with remorse because I understood that he did care awfully about the war. Then he spoiled it by saying, "War's a terrible business, my dear. Here's your Churchill sending a thousand bombers to attack Cologne, one of the most beautiful cities in the world."

Just as if it wasn't a German city at all, and anyway, it can't be more beautiful than London. Or Bath.

Then Grandmother dropped her own bomb. "So we want you to go to the country and stay with your other grandmother."

"No! Oh, Gran!"

"Not want, Margaret. We don't *want* her to go. Poor child'll begin to think . . . you know . . . pillar to post."

"Of course not want, dear. I didn't mean *want*."

"Well, you chose an extremely unfortunate word I must say."

"Gran, why can't I stay here?"

"I agree, George, it could have been better expressed. Kate, dear . . ."

"Certainly could!"

"Kate dear, your grandfather and I feel it would be best. Best for you, that is, if you were to go to stay with your father's mother for a while. Your other grandmother. In the country."

"But why?"

"That's better. In a nutshell! There, that's settled, then. I'm going to need some more yellow pins now, Margaret."

Some nutshell! I took a long deep breath and tried to hush the angry voice that was screaming inside me: will you both please pull yourselves together and stop arguing and cross-talking and tell me *why*, just when I think I might be able to settle in at that ghastly school and get to know a couple of those ghastly girls, you suddenly decide I can't stay here and have to be shoved off to the country to stay with that ghastly old woman?

"I'm sure you'll love it there, dear."

"Why?"

"Well, it's—well, it's country. Plenty of trees."

"No, I meant why do I have to go?"

"Mind you, she'll miss the harbor, won't you dear?"

"Oh yes, Grandfather, I certainly shall. But why do I have to go?"

"Submarines!"

"Exactly!" Horrors, things must be serious, I thought, they're agreeing on something.

"It'll be bombs next, you mark my words. I'll need a lot more yellow."

"And those kamikaze pilots. The ones that suicide. I couldn't face your mother if anything should happen to you, dear."

"Anything happened to her here, you probably wouldn't be spared yourself, Margaret. Nor me either. We're front line now, you know."

"I wouldn't mind, really I wouldn't," I blithered. "I'd much rather stay here with you. And Grandfather's right, you know, how on earth could I explain to Mummy if you were bombed out here and I was safe in the country?" Safe! With Grandmother Tucker! What crazy words were these! "And anyway, I can't possibly go to stay with that woman. Really I can't." I hoped I wasn't going to cry.

"Don't cry, dear." Grandmother was infuriatingly sympathetic. "We honestly feel it's for the best. Your grandfather talked it over with the others at the bowling club."

Oh well, that's it then. They'd know everything, those men at the bowling club.

As if he'd heard me Grandpa murmured, "Yes, they're a pretty cluey lot at the bowling club."

"Quite a few people are thinking of sending their children to the country. I don't know why you're so upset. It'll be just like when your mother had to send you to Burnham-on-Sea—and you loved Mrs. Poole, now didn't you?"

That was different. I was younger then. And Mrs. Poole was a darling farmer's wife with rosy cheeks, she wasn't my Grandmother Tucker. Again the uncanny old man seemed to read my thoughts.

"She wasn't your Grandmother Tucker, mind."

"Well no, George, she wasn't. But we're very fortunate to have Grandmother Tucker available, aren't we?"

23

Oh yes, let's by all means look on the bright side. Dear jolly old Grandmother Tucker. We're certainly fortunate having her available.

"She most probably won't have me anyway."

"Oh yes, she'll have you. I telephoned today. You're booked on Thursday's train."

The two days that followed were absolute and utter hell. The complete futility of trying to get either of my grandparents to listen to me was the worst part of it all. They were so smugly sure that they were doing the very best thing for me and wouldn't consider my point of view. Whenever I tried to raise the subject Grandpa would go off on one of his own little conversational saunters where no one could possibly follow, and Grandmother would tighten her lips and murmur comforting words.

"I'm sure Grandmother Tucker is just longing to see you, dear. As I was."

"But you don't know her."

"And to have you stay with her."

"You've never met her! Have you? Never even met her!"

"It's for your own good, darling. Look, I tell you what. Why don't we go to the cinema tonight? Douglas Fairbanks in *The Corsican Brothers*. You'd love him."

"She hates us! You know that, don't you? Hates us!"

"Oh come, hate's a strong word, darling."

"Well, she does. She's not normal. You're sending me to live with a weird woman, do you realize that?"

"Katharine dear, she's perfectly normal. I'm sure. Her world may be different from ours, but of course she's normal. And I'm sure her heart's in the right place."

24

It wasn't her heart I was worried about so much as her head. From what I'd heard my mother say, Grandmother Tucker's head was a long way out of kilter.

"Grandmother, do listen. She hates me!"

"Of course she doesn't. What nonsense Kate. It's your mother she . . . she doesn't hate anyone."

"Yes, she hates my mother too. And my father. Both of them she hates. And me."

"Now, dear, let's have no more of this silly talk. Would you rather see Charlie Chaplin in *The Great Dictator*? It's at the Savoy . . ."

So I tackled Grandfather when Grandmother was safely out of the place at her Red Cross meeting. He made even less sense than she did.

"Oh, she's a funny one, Kate. There's no doubt of that. No doubt at all."

I hadn't said there was. But funny? It wasn't the word I would have used.

"But I think she's sound enough," he added.

I *knew* she wasn't. Sound she was not. And she certainly wasn't funny either.

"Don't know much about the family, I admit," he said. "A reclusive old lady by the sound of it. Never comes to Sydney, or if she does she doesn't get in touch with your grandmother or me. Immensely wealthy, of course. Husband, a local solicitor. Old family. Died tragically in the Great War. Do you know, young Kate, that on a morning in August 1915, two hundred and thirty-four Australian Light Horsemen were killed in an area no bigger than your suburban tennis court? True! Your Grandfather Tucker was one of those. Sadly mismanaged, that whole campaign." And he shook his head and went across to gloom at his map and move a few pins around. Wishing he'd been at Gallipoli to manage it properly for them, I suppose. I will admit that Grandpa was well up on his wars.

"It's a very pleasant little place, I believe, Parsons Creek, and of course she lives very well, all the comforts. None of the alarms and excursions we're suffering here. That's the trouble with folk in the country. They don't know there's a war on."

"People in *this* country don't," I whined. "There's no danger here, Grandpa, truly."

He staggered back as if I'd hit him.

"Compared to England, I mean. Of course I know there's danger here, in Sydney, *here*, with you . . ." blithering again.

"I suspect it's the food that makes the difference, you know."

"What?"

"Food. Shortages. People in the country don't suffer as much as we do, you see. Fresh eggs, butter, plenty of that sort of thing. Cushions the blow quite a bit, a farm-fresh egg."

"Grandpa, please don't make me go!"

"We'll have the roses back in your cheeks in no time at all."

His mind was still on farm produce. He made me sound like a convalescent and suddenly I felt like one too. So I gave up. When old Grandmother Tucker murdered me they'd be sorry, and what would they tell my mother then? Whatever they told her, I'm sure she wouldn't be able to understand what they were talking about any more than I could.

5

Linda's intervention had worked wonders on the morning lines and no one commented as I slunk on to the end of 3A the next day. I'd thought it best to spend recess in the library as usual, not wanting to seem too eager for company. Miss Carpenter would have missed me if I hadn't turned up. I mourned to think what her life would be like when I went to stay with my other grandmother. She might offer to adopt me if she knew. I couldn't bring myself to tell her I was leaving and felt guilty all the time she smiled at me from her desk. I said a specially hearty "Good-bye then, Miss Carpenter," as I put *Rambles in the Yorkshire Dales* back on her table, and wondered if she'd do herself in from loneliness when she found I'd gone for good.

At lunchtime I used the same ploy that had worked the day before and sure enough Linda paused at the door and wagged her head in my direction. I was in! I had friends! Hooray! Too late, of course.

Lunch wasn't easy. They seemed to think I'd been frightened by the submarine attack and had demanded to be sent even farther away from the firing line. I had to admit it sounded fishy. First I'd run from the bombing in London and now at the first sign of danger I was running again. They took a lot of convincing. I would have liked their advice about Grandma Tucker, but it didn't seem loyal to discuss members of one's family with friends of only a day. Well, it was two days now, but it still seemed oversoon to tell them how horrid my paternal grandmother had been to my parents, and how much I dreaded going to live with her.

That afternoon at the tram shed there was a sad farewell scene. Not entirely on my account, I will admit. Cathy was uncharacteristically subdued. Her sister's American boyfriend's buddy had taken another girl out the night before and it looked as if Cathy might have to wait awhile longer for romance to blossom. I condoled with her, but her problems were nothing compared with mine.

So there we were, back in a taxi crossing the harbor bridge again, this time on our way to Central Railway Station. I'd said good-bye to the other people in the block of flats and every one of them assured me that I'd be much safer in the country. Not one of them had ever met my Grandmother Tucker.

Before the taxi came Grandmother, sniffing and red of eye, presented me with a gift, a brown leather handbag with a silver snap on the top and a square mirror backed with leather inside the side pocket. There was a purse to match and in that Grandfather placed five one-pound notes.

"Insurance money, my dear"—and he and Grandmother chortled as if it was the funniest thing anyone had ever said. Grandpa Dawson had been manager of a big insurance company before he retired, so I guess it was an old family joke. Then Grandmother took me aside and handed me an envelope with *Mrs. R. Tucker* written across the front in a very spidery handwriting, and below it, *11 Park Street, Parsons Creek, N.S.W.*

"A letter for your grandmother," she said. It was sealed, so I'd have to wait until I arrived at Parsons Creek before I could steam it open and read it. My mother told me once that it was good manners not to seal letters when you give them to someone to post or deliver. Pity Grandma Dawson hadn't been told how to behave. Then she fished another envelope from the pocket of her jacket.

"This is for a gift," she whispered, "for your grand-mother."

"Why don't you send her something?" I whispered back in a pleading tone.

"No, no. Much better if you buy her something. She wouldn't welcome . . ."

"Oh please, please, dear Gran. I don't want to buy her a present, she hates me!" And I'm working up a prodigious dislike of her as well. "I shan't know what to buy. Truly!"

"You'll think of something, dear. Some little thing to please her."

I didn't care about pleasing her. She'd never sent me so much as a birthday card in my entire life. Once again I bleated that Grandma Tucker didn't want to have me stay with her.

"Of course she does, darling, she's very happy to have you."

"Did she say that?" She hadn't. Grandma Dawson was lying.

"Very happy. It's just that . . . if I were to send her anything she might be offended."

I knew when I was beaten; she was determined to

29

tell me nothing. So I let her slide the second envelope into the other side of the new handbag and snap shut the lid. Now the brown leather receptacle was ready for a journey even if I wasn't. It held my train ticket, a clean handkerchief, the mirror and purse and the two envelopes. It also contained a large square piece of cardboard which I wouldn't let Grandfather tie on the outside, and to her credit Grandmother backed me up. It had my name printed on it and PASSENGER TO PARSONS CREEK and the Kirribilli address too. Printed in bright blue crayon. Like a name tag some people put on their dogs. I planned to jettison it out of the train window as soon as we were clear of Sydney.

Central Station was small compared to the London stations I knew, but just as busy. There was khaki and navy blue everywhere, kitbags to trip over and loud and garbled messages adding to the din of hissing steam trains. Grandfather left Gran and me waiting under the big clock in the center of the main concourse while he tottered off to the kiosk. He came back with a packet of mints for me and an insultingly juvenile comic book which Gran made him take back and exchange for the threepenny *Women's Weekly*. I thought it very decent of her, specially since she was well into the sobbing stage now. I wished again, ever so strongly, that I wasn't leaving them.

Then, in spite of every effort I could muster, I began to cry. The tears had such a magical effect that I regretted my past stoicism. Grandfather swallowed, turned away and blew his nose and Grandmother hugged me close and whispered: "Please, darling, try it. Just for a month. You've a return ticket that expires in one month, and if it's too bad of course you must come back to me."

Just for a month! So the sentence was not for the term of my natural life after all. If I could manage for four weeks then I might come back to Sydney, unless of course I expired along with my ticket just as the four weeks were up. It was the best concession I could hope for. So we bawled our way along the platform to my carriage and Grandpa bustled in and found the seat he'd booked for me. It was a window seat, of course, facing forward. Grandfather would have accepted nothing less, war or no war. They settled me in and Grandmother handed over the brown-paper bag she'd brought with food for the journey. There were others in the carriage and I was embarrassed. My grandparents kissed me again and stepped down to the platform just as the whistle sounded and the train huffed and puffed and started to move. Grandmother found time to glare sternly at the two soldiers in the compartment, and to advise me quite loudly to Be Careful! Grandmother Dawson was completely convinced that all men in uniform Wanted Only One Thing, and she was quite determined that they shouldn't get it. Certainly not from me!

6

I stood at the carriage door and waved until I could see them no more, then I settled down on the leather seat that already smelled of orange peel and apple cores. An elderly couple had the window seats on the other side of the carriage and as soon as the train moved they both seemed to fall fast asleep. Probably didn't want to talk to the rest of us, the two soldiers and me. They were privates in felty khaki uniforms. The one opposite me couldn't have been more than sixteen. He had coarse greasy hair and lots of pimples. The uniform made him look thick and lumpy. The other one was much more handsome but it was a while before I knew it. It wasn't only my grandmother's recent farewell remark, my mother had warned me so alarmingly about the hazards of speaking to servicemen that I was scared even to peep lest one of these should pounce on me with evil intent. But I did take a good look when I could see from the corner of my eye that he was staring out of the other window. He had fair hair, soft and flossy, and blue eyes, like Rupert Brooke. I just knew he'd write poetry. His skin was clear and pale and even the felty uniform sat well on him. He turned suddenly and grinned and winked at me, so I gave him a chilling stare and opened my *Women's Weekly*, wishing I was old enough to wear lipstick.

At the first stop the soldiers got out and ran along beside the train banging on the doors and shouting to someone called Chilla. They must have found him because they didn't come back. The old couple came awake then and nodded and smiled at me, but I didn't want to talk and stayed with my magazine, with an occasional glance at the countryside as it slid by the window. The best part of it was at the beginning. We crossed a river and chugged along beside it for a while and the views were beautiful, but soon I found it better not to look. Depressing miles of fields, paddocks they call them here, stretched away into the distance, and pole after pole dizzied me as they flashed by. It was stuffy in the carriage but when I opened the window nearest me just a little, the old lady started to cough and splutter and the old man glared, so I closed it again and took the mirror from my handbag. No change. Exactly the same number of spots that I'd set out with, the same pale straight hair, blue eyes with dark circles under them, shiny nose and fat lips. I checked that my ticket was still there, particularly the return half, then replaced the mirror and pondered my sorry situation.

According to what my mother had told me, Grandmother Tucker was both wicked and mean. Ever since Grandfather Tucker's death in the First War she'd lived alone in the old family mansion with servants to look after her and nothing to do except count her money. She hated my mother—Mummy had told me that herself, more than once. She quite desperately hadn't wanted my father to marry anyone, and when he and Mummy

33

fell in love, Grandma Tucker had carried on something fierce and said Mummy wasn't good enough for him. But they'd married anyway and my father had decided that he had to go as far away as he possibly could in case his mother did some harm to Mummy, so he'd taken her to England and made a solemn promise that she'd never have to come back to Australia and face his mother, ever again. What my poor parents would suffer when the Dawsons told them that they'd sent me actually to live with her was too terrible to think about. I wished now that I'd asked my parents more questions about her, but Parsons Creek had seemed so far away from London and the chance of ever meeting her wildly remote.

I ended up feeling so sorry for myself that even the good old *Women's Weekly* couldn't keep my thoughts from drifting back to the unfairness of it all, so I got myself a drink of cold water from the squat, heavy glass decanter that stood on its shelf on the wall by the door. It tasted of metal and soot, but I had to drink the whole glass full because I didn't dare open the window again to throw it out. Then to my relief the old lady took sandwiches from her big tapestry holdall and offered me one. Hers were in a brown-paper bag too, so I was able to refuse politely and open my own.

Making sandwiches was a talent my grandmother did not possess. Along with setting breakfast tables. I suppose all those tasks had been done by the maid who'd joined the WRANS, practically over Grandmother's dead body, at the start of the war. Grandmother never spoke about her directly, but I often heard her moaning "Oh Edith, Edith," as she struggled with one of the household chores, and Grandpa had told me who Edith was when I asked him. A veritable treasure and one of the reasons they'd sold their big house and moved into the flat. There was no doubt that no matter how much her husband seemed to be enjoying it, Grandmother Dawson would be a lot happier when the war was over. So also would the people who had to eat her untasty sandwiches. There was an apple as well, but I couldn't eat that, of course, because of the smell and the crunching noise. The old couple were nibbling at their dainty little triangles without making the slightest sound and when they finished they closed their eyes and slept again. I folded my brown-paper bag as quietly as I could and stowed it on the luggage rack above my head. Maybe some hungry passenger would find it later and profit from the apple.

It was one o'clock by my wristwatch; we'd be there at ten past two. Grandpa had explained to me the necessity of watching the time during the journey, because although the station master would call out the name of the town when the train pulled in, all station signs had been taken down, just as they had in England, to confuse enemy paratroopers. I consider that any enemy who was smart enough to get into the country would most likely have the sense to bring a few maps with him, but Grandpa said no, it was always one of the first things you must do in a war, take down all the signs at railway stations.

The dozing couple woke again as we pulled into another nameless station. The old lady smiled at me. Her skin and hair were dead-white and her eyes very pale, but when she smiled she looked quite young and frisky.

"Going far, are you, dear?"

"To Parsons Creek, to stay with my grandmother. We arrive there at ten past two." I smiled at her, but carefully; my lips are even fatter if I do a full smile.

"Well I never, you're English, aren't you?" I hadn't thought my accent was as obvious as all that. "Dad, I say Dad, the little girl here's English. What you think of that?"

So Dad turned and smiled at me too. "Fancy that, English, eh? Fancy that."

"She's come a long way. I say you've come a long way, love."

I found their conversation fell short of being stimulating, but they were trying to make me feel welcome, so I told them about coming out to live with the Dawson grands at Kirribilli and of course that gave the old gent the opportunity to ask me what I thought of the harbor. I don't think I've met one single person who hasn't asked me that. So, using my sincerest voice, I said I adored it and should miss it terribly when I was at Parsons Creek. I said the name loudly and clearly, hoping they might know it and be able to tell me about it, and possibly something of my grandmother. But they were going farther west and didn't know the town at all.

They asked how things were in England and how I'd got out to Australia. I told them and didn't spare any awful details, so they wouldn't feel they'd wasted their time by talking to me. I could have gone on, but the telegraph poles were moving more slowly now past the window, and I knew we were nearing my destination.

A great circular wheat silo went by, then an enormous shed with no sides, for storing grain, I supposed, then the houses of the town, mostly weatherboard with corrugated tin roofs, water tanks beside them and tiny outhouse lavs in their backyards.

The old man jumped up to help me with my suitcase and he was so tiny that he had to stand on the seat to

36

reach it. I was mortified because I could easily have done it myself but I didn't know how to stop him. I picked up the *Women's Weekly*, for there were some bits I hadn't read, then I offered it to the old lady who snatched it gladly and got right into it. They probably slept so much because their conversation was so boring.

By this time the train was nearing the station and I sat down again and leaned my cheek against the window to see along the platform. I'd begun to feel a faint tingle of anticipatory pleasure, certainly not at the prospect of meeting my grandmother, but of sampling some really rich living for a while.

As we slid along to a stop I checked out the people waiting. There was an elderly man holding a small dog in his arms, two girls a bit older than me, jumping up and down, giggling and pointing, a young woman holding a baby, and the stationmaster in black trousers, black waistcoat and rolled-up shirt-sleeves. There was also a young porter in charge of a vee-shaped trolley that he was wheeling very importantly toward the guard's van at the back of the train.

The old man grappled with the door handle and finally got it open for me. Before I could finish saying good-bye to him and his wife, the two young soldiers who had been in the carriage when we set off raced up the platform, jumped into the carriage, grabbed their topcoats and kit bags from the luggage rack, and jumped out again.

I followed.

7

There was no one there to meet me. The station-master called "Parsons Creek" up and down the plat-form, but no one came to greet me. A gray-haired man stepped down from another carriage and the elderly man with the dog smiled and walked forward. They clasped hands and the dog's ears were fondled, then they walked away together. The two girls shrieked and ran to the two soldiers, who dropped their coats and kit bags and swept them around in a big swinging circle, then kissed them hard and long. Then they picked up their stuff and sauntered off, each with an arm around a simpering girl. They looked awfully stupid, but I en-vied the girls their clear unspotty complexions, bright red lips and shiny hair, rolled up in sleek brown sausages around their heads. I'd been planning to cut mine as soon as I was well away from Grandmother Dawson, who was a staunch believer in plaits for young girls, but now I thought I might try rolling it a bit to see how it looked. Grandmother Tucker would probably have a lady's maid who could help me with it.

The woman with the baby came toward me and for

a minute I thought she might have been sent as a welcoming party, but she just muttered crossly, "Move, willya? There's people gotta get on, ya know."

So I moved myself and my suitcase and she climbed into the compartment I had left. Doors banged, the stationmaster blew a sharp whistle, the porter trundled past pushing his queer conveyance, which now held a few parcels and a large crate with holes in the sides.

The train slipped away. I waved to the old couple, picked up my case, and stood there alone, wondering when the next train was due so that I could throw myself under its wheels if it was going west and leap on board if it was heading back to Sydney. By now the only other person left on the platform was the stationmaster, standing by the exit gate with his hand out, waiting to be given my ticket, I supposed. I marched across, plonked my case down, opened my handbag and handed him the forward half. Then in my most sophisticated voice I asked directions to Park Street. There was a faint hope he might have a message for me. (Been held up . . . look after the dear child until I can get there . . . make her feel welcome . . . give her tea . . . tell her I'm so looking forward to meeting her.) He had no such message.

"Straight down the main street there, then second on your left."

I hefted my valise and set off. Past the stationmaster's house just by the station yard, the Railway Hotel opposite, then some vacant land, several small shops and a stock-and-station agency. A few motorcars were parked along the street at an angle with their noses facing the roadway. Not many people were about. There was no sign of the soldiers and their girlfriends, but the two elderly men strolled along about half a block ahead of me. The one who had come on the train was now holding the dog and his companion carried a small suitcase. It was a beautiful bag, elegantly shaped and covered in wine-colored velvet. I would have swapped it gladly for my scratched and battered heavy leather one. Grandmother had thoughtfully wedged a layer of schoolbooks into it, just in case I felt the urge to study, and my arm ached already from carrying it. I crossed the first street to another hotel, the Royal this time, and across from it the Clubhouse. Obviously there was no need ever to be thirsty in Parsons Creek. Then there were more shops, and the next corner, Park Street. I decided to slow down just in case I'd missed something interesting. So I turned and went back to the first cross-street.

Next door to the Royal Hotel was a milk bar. It glittered and shone, all white and blue and silver, with a sign above the footpath saying White Rose Café. Suddenly I was dying for a drink so I walked through the door. I put my bag down beside one of the tables and then went across to the counter. A young man was standing behind it polishing glasses. He glared at me. He was the most ferocious person I'd ever seen, with thick black hair, heavy eyebrows that almost met across the top of his nose, and a swarthy complexion. He'd obviously taken an instant dislike to me and I wished I hadn't chosen his stupid milk bar for my drink, but otherwise there seemed to be only public houses in this stupid town.

With the habit I have of trying to ingratiate myself with people who don't appear to like me, I bleated, "Your shop is very pleasant . . . outside . . . and in too, of course . . ."

He intensified his glare and muttered, "Yes?"

"I mean . . . it sparkles . . . really sparkles. Oh, sorry. A milk shake. Caramel, please."

He lifted one of the round metal lids off its place in the countertop and ladled milk into one of the shiny metal beakers. Then he measured out the caramel flavoring from the row of upside-down bottles, put in a scoop of ice cream from under another metal lid and was just about to clamp the whole lot onto the machine to froth it up when I suddenly heard my voice say, "Could you make it a malted, please? A caramel malted milk does seem much more spiffy, doesn't it?"

"Does it?" He grunted, and flicked the malted milk powder by the spoonful from its jar. He was so boorish that a memory came back to me of something I'd seen my mother do once, and had completely forgotten until now. She waited until the man had made up two milk shakes, one for her and one for me. I remember I'd asked for a chocolate one and was profoundly looking forward to drinking it. Then she said, "We don't want them, thank you. You were insolent to me." And she took my hand and we walked out of the shop. He was a Cockney, and I remember feeling terribly tiny and scared and sick as we marched down the road away from his place with him shouting after us in his loud voice with no *t*'s in it: "Wo's va ma'er wif you ven? Wo' a lo' a rubbish!"

The worst part of the memory is that I agreed with him. I thought my mother was being unreasonable. He'd just been a bit grumpy, but I didn't have the courage to say so. And I had been looking forward to that chocolate milk shake.

I waited until the machine had whirled all the ingredients to his satisfaction. He held the metal container high above the expectant glass, fluted and polished and clear, and poured the malted milk down into it in a long pale-brown stream, then set it, frothing, on the counter in front of me. Then he said, "Sparkles? Why shouldn't it sparkle? I wash and polish that glass out there every day, don't I?"

There were straws in a metal container on the counter so I took one and dipped it into the icy sweetness. It was the very best malted I'd ever tasted, but I decided not to tell him.

"Every day," he hissed at me, "every single morning. What do you think of that, eh?"

I sucked furiously, my eyes steady on the froth. He looked foreign and the white rose was the flower of Athens, so I presumed he was Greek. But that didn't explain why he was so crabby with me. Goodness knows I'd done my best to be pleasant! So I finished the glass quickly, poured in the rest from the metal container, scooped out the blob of ice cream that was stuck on the base, and ended up with a very satisfactory slurp as my straw struck bottom. He kept on glaring. I fingered one of the pound notes from my purse and paid him. He crashed the price up on the till and gave me one ten-shilling note, four florins, a shilling and some coppers, but no smile or good-bye. I picked up my suitcase and set off once more. He'd looked just a bit older than me and I had thought at least he might be friendly.

I plodded along the street. Next to the milk bar was a fruit shop, then a butcher, then a big general store that took up most of the rest of the block. On the corner was a bank and that was the corner of Park Street and I really couldn't put it off any longer. I had to turn the corner and find my grandmother's house.

I turned. The first few houses I passed were built of wood, weatherboard, some painted, some just weathered. Then I came to number eleven. I stopped.

This one was built of bricks. And each brick had been

painted so that no two in a row were the same color. It was a tiny house and all the colors were bright primary: red, yellow, and blue, with cunning mixtures here and there that caught the eye and startled it. It was an extremely garish house, but the paint had been on a long time and was flaking on some of the bricks, and instead of looking gay and happy it had a sad, decrepit appearance. It was not the mansion I had expected to see. There must be some mistake.

8

As I stood there trying to decide between a quick death on the railway track and a confrontation with the occupant of this house, the curtain at the front window of the house next door twitched. Someone was watching me. When I turned, the curtain was back in place. I could think of no reason why my grandmother's neighbor should spy on me—if this was my grandmother's house, which of course it wasn't. I looked around. On the opposite side of the street was a small park, empty of people but crammed full of park furniture: metal seats, a pretty bandstand with cast-iron lace around it and a tall white marble war memorial with a long list of names painted in gold. There was no one else in the whole street but me. I checked the address on the envelope in my handbag: *11 Park Street, Parsons Creek, N.S.W.*

And now it was starting to rain, not a sudden downpour but a light, insistent drizzle guaranteed to wet you through to the bone eventually. My feet wanted to run to the bandstand for shelter, but, weird as it may seem, my father wouldn't let them go. Suddenly I could hear his voice and it was just as I'd been trying to remember it all these months. I could feel a goofy smile opening my face as I listened.

"Be still," it said, so I was still; the only thing I did was breathe. And drip.

"Now think," it said, so I thought. But my thinking provided no answers to my problems. Why had I been given the wrong address? Why hadn't my grandmother met the train? And who lived in this peculiar little house anyway? But Father's influence was strong and I was able to pick up my suitcase and open the gate and walk firmly up the path to the door. I'd come so far now there was no sense in turning round, and what would I tell the Dawsons if I took the next train back to Sydney?

"Be still. Now think." I'd heard my father saying that for ages. Mainly to my mother, who has the habit of flying into panics and racing about in all directions at once before she works out what she's panicking about. Since I'd come to live with her parents I felt I knew where she'd got it from. Honestly, if my mother comes to a door she never thinks to turn the handle, she sort of beats at it, thinking it's going to open because it somehow knows she's there. She also cries a lot, which I find irritating. She just never tries being a stoic, and no one else can get on with fixing the problem that caused the tears, because Mummy has to be hushed up first. So when I told the girls at school and the old people on the train about the Blitz and the nights in the Underground, I was making it sound a lot cheerier than in fact it was. I mean, I was scared stiff myself, but it really did help to sing with the others and to laugh together at the dopey jokes. But Mummy, always keeping a tight and sweaty grip on my hand, wouldn't join in anything. Well, actually she couldn't, because all the time she kept up a sort of low keening noise. She swore she couldn't help it, but it put the rest of us off our singing, I can tell you that. I certainly missed my father when he went into the RAF.

Whoever owned this house had odd ideas about landscaping. On my way up the path I had to run the gauntlet of a large army of identical garden gnomes, lined up in rows like trees in an orchard. Their tiny green feet were set firmly on cement and their jaunty caps stood out like little red windsocks caught in a gale-force wind. They had smiling mouths but beady eyes that didn't look too friendly. I made it safely to the front door and there was another gnome, this one a huge brass knocker with a beard that crashed noisily against the top button of his shirt, but brought no answer from inside the house.

I banged that beard again and again. No one came to the door, but with the force of my fifth bang it swung open. I was still, listening, for a moment, then I swung it wider and walked into the house.

I put my bag down just inside the front door in case a quick getaway was needed, then stamped loudly down the central hallway, peeping into the rooms on either side as I passed. The curtains were closed and there was a strong smell of furniture polish coming from the front room on the right. I could see a sofa and two chairs with white doilies on each arm, and a fireplace with a large bowl of red paper flowers blazing from the mantel above it. There was no blaze below; the fireplace itself was filled with pinecones. The chairs and sofa were covered in dark-blue brocadey stuff and had cushions so smooth that it seemed no human contact had ever been made with them. This must be the parlor, I thought, and turned to look into the room opposite. And tottered with astonishment.

It was a bedroom. There was a narrow bed with a bright patchwork coverlet, a wide wardrobe, but above all the room had the appearance of an alarmingly overstocked secondhand bookstall! There were books everywhere, in piles on the floor, on top of the wardrobe, and I guessed inside it too, stacked on the armchair by the bed and lined up along the windowsill. It was pleasing to see books, I like books, but there were so many of them, so carelessly strewn about, that a lot of my pleasure in seeing them was diminished by the thought of someone having to tidy them up sometime.

The next room on the right was the bathroom—I knew because I could smell disinfectant and coldness. A door at the end of the passage opened onto what seemed to be a back veranda, with another room off that, and to the left was the kitchen. In the center of the kitchen stood a long pine table, scratched and worn, and six chairs with high backs. There was an enormous sideboard along one wall and a low cupboard with a terrazzo sink above it on another. The back wall held a big black fuel stove. The door of the stove was open and a tiny flame was struggling to survive in there. It was a warm and welcoming room, except that there was no one there to welcome me.

I stood in the doorway feeling suddenly desolate, unutterably lonely, more lonely than I'd felt in all the time since I'd said good-bye to my mother and father.

I heard footsteps, the back door of the veranda creaked open and bashed closed. And there, standing in the doorway with an armload of firewood, was the most alarmingly dilapidated old woman I had ever seen. She was thin, her bones almost glowing through her skin.

She had a big mouth—my mouth, but startlingly full of large teeth, the fiercest blue eyes—my father's eyes, with ferocity added, and wispy gray hair pulled back into a tight little knob at the back of her head and tied with a bright red ribbon. She wore a navy blue ribbed sweater that seemed big enough for two of her, and beneath that a voluminous skirt that looked for all the world like a tablecloth my mother had at home. Green-and-blue checks with strawberries in the checks. It came right down to the tops of her white tennis shoes.

I looked back at her face and found she'd only just arrived at my feet, so I waited until she looked up too.

"So you've arrived," she said. "Took your time, didn't you?"

"I stopped for a milkshake."

"Ah, yes, that'd be at the White Rose." And she burst into loud laughter. I didn't laugh, just waited. Then she said: "Well, come on then, child, put a couple of these on the fire. I've a dinner to cook."

I took the firewood from her arms and then didn't know where to put it, but there was a wooden box on the hearth that looked likely so I shoved it in there and pushed two smallish pieces into the top of the brave little flame.

Then I brushed my hands together and turned back to her. "Hello, Grandmother," I said, in a voice that came out much smaller than I had intended. "I'm Katharine."

She stared into my face with her cobalt eyes. "Yes," she said, "I can see you are. You've the look of your father at . . . how old are you now, fourteen?"

They always think I'm younger, adults. I suppose it's because I'm not very tall, and the hair, of course.

"I'm fifteen and a half, actually. Am I really like my father?"

"How would I know," she snapped. "You look as he used to look, but as for *being* like him, how would I know? You've only just got here. Did you bring anything?"

What on earth should I have brought? I wondered if she meant presents and was about to open my purse and give her the money that Grandma Dawson had put there, then I realized that of course she meant identification. So I opened the purse anyway and fished out the Dawsons' letter and handed it to her. I felt annoyed because I hadn't had a chance to steam it open and read it. But she just shoved it up onto the mantel where it would be lost forever because there were so many other things cluttering the space up there.

"I mean luggage. You bring any with you? Leave it at the station? Belongings? Clothes?"

I felt about two years old, and stupid as well, and that made me as angry as Grandmother Tucker seemed to be.

I glared back at her. "Yes, I did bring some luggage. I left it by the front door. Which was open, by the way."

She nodded. "Always is."

"Well, do you think that's wise? I mean, anyone could walk right into your house, couldn't they?"

She just said, "Yes," very calmly, and somehow I felt that was the end of that line of conversation.

"You can put your stuff in the front bedroom," she went on. "You unpack while I get on with the tea." And she turned her back on me and rattled things about on the top of the stove. I wandered back down the hallway, collected my suitcase and dumped it on the bed in the front room. Then I took it off the bed and put it on the floor, because the bedspread was made up of thousands of tiny different-colored squares, all sewn together by hand and it really was like a glorious stained-

49

glass window; it seemed a shame to mess it up too much. There was room in the wardrobe for my things so I unpacked and pushed the case under the bed. I was tempted to stay packed and ready to go in case the chance to escape cropped up soon, but my grandmother looked the type of person it would be very hard to lie to, and she'd probably come and snoop to see if I'd done as I was told.

It seemed prudent to stay there until she called me, so I put some of the books from the chair onto the floor and sat down.

There really were enough books on the floor of that bedroom to stock a library! They were all beautifully bound, some with soft leather, and inside the cover of each was a small, elegant bookplate. It was what I think they call a woodcut and showed a doorway with a large octagonal knob in the center and above it a knocker in the form of a lion's head. There were intricate leadlight panels in the door and down each side. It was a grand and interesting door, but what was more interesting was that beneath the door on the bookplate was printed in Gothic script "Ex Libris Charles Hope."

I checked a few more books, and sure enough, each of them had the same bookplate and the same name on it. I'd heard of rich people who wanted to own books but didn't know much about them, so bought up someone else's library, and I guessed Grandmother Tucker must be one of these. Or else a thief.

She called, "Tea's ready," and I went back reluctantly to the kitchen. The table was set with a long strip of cloth—the same material as the skirt she was wearing—laid across it, making a place for each of us on opposite sides. She noticed that I noticed and said, "Saw you admiring my skirt. Well, this is more of the same.

Tablecloth it was, far too big for one person, so I put it to better use."

I began to tell her that my mother had one like it, only she still used hers as a tablecloth, but she interrupted me as soon as I began.

"Now there's one thing you better get straight before we start. I've certain strong beliefs and the one right on top of the list is that children should be seen and not heard. So while you live with me, you'll speak only when spoken to. You prepared to accept that?"

I didn't see that I had any choice really so I said, "Yes, but . . ." and she cut me off by bobbing her head with the red ribbon up and down and saying very firmly, "Right. Now we understand each other. Button your lip."

Then she served up a very decent meal with lots of vegetables, cooked together, with slices of bacon on top, all crispy and with a rind you could chew right up. She picked hers up in her fingers to chew the rind so I did the same. Just as I'd got a good mouthful she almost choked me by saying, "Friend of mine killed last week."

"Killed? Wha . . . who?" I spluttered.

"A pig, of course." And I felt two years old again.

To follow there was a round loaf, a sort of soda bread that she called damper, and a pot of the most delicious honey I'd ever seen or tasted. It had pieces of beeswax in it and I swear I could have eaten the whole jar in one go. We had mugs of tea with that and then Grandma, who'd been staring at me all through the meal, stood up.

"Hmm. You might have the makings of something there," she said. "We'll see. You can give me a hand to clear this lot up now."

So we cleared and washed, me being very careful not

51

to say a word. Well, I did try to chat a couple of times, but she just wouldn't answer—so she really did mean it about being seen and not heard. I could see the next month was going to be a very trying period of my life.

When the kitchen was all tidy she stared intently into my eyes and said, "You'll be wanting a brick."

A brick. I stood very still and wondered why on earth I should need a brick, especially at that hour of night. Fortunately she didn't seem to require an answer. She bustled across to the sideboard and from the bottom shelf withdrew an old newspaper, large sheets like the London *Times* with columns and columns of classifieds on the front page.

"Very well worth buying, the *Herald*," she said. "Comes in useful for so many things." And she spread the paper on the kitchen table, then grabbed an oven cloth and from the back of the stove she pulled out an ordinary house brick. Was it hot! She flew back to the table, dumped it on a corner of the paper and wrapped it up snugly like a parcel. Then she picked it up and handed it to me.

"There you are. Pop it in your bed straightaway, but mind you don't leave your feet on it too long, you'll get chilblains."

I dashed along the hall with my radiant bundle and popped it as directed, then I slid back into the kitchen in case Grandma had anything else to say. She hadn't, but I watched as she parceled her own brick. For a rich lady she certainly lived in an extremely frugal manner.

When it was done she tucked it under her arm and said, "Well, I'm off to bed then. We might have a talk in the morning. Good night." And she toddled off through the door, calling back at me, "Turn the light off after you."

Then suddenly she was in the doorway again, looking at me. I took a chance and inquired, "Where do you sleep?"

She nodded her head to show that her room was behind the kitchen fireplace wall, off the back veranda. At least I'd got a sort of answer, and it seemed a good time to get a bit more information from her, but I couldn't think of what to ask her first, and by now she was glaring quite ferociously at me.

"Good night," I muttered, then pulled the cord that switched off the light, and we both set off to bed in opposite directions.

Mine was a comfortable bed and there was a bed lamp screwed to the windowsill beside it, but I didn't dare read in case that was another rule of the house. No reading in bed. It was in our house back home. Mummy was sure I'd be stark raving blind by the time I was twenty because I read in bed so much. She'd even taken my reading lamp away once and then carried on as if she had rabies because she caught me reading with a torch under the blankets.

Anyway, I was too tired to read this night, so I put off thinking about my sorry situation and went right off to sleep.

9

The gnomes had come alive! I could hear them scraping and scritching tiny feet free of their concrete bases and tittering and whispering in high-pitched, hissing, secretive voices, scuffling and sliding as they scurried around the side of my grandmother's house.

I crept from under the blankets and ran barefoot down the cold linoleum of the hallway to the back of the house. I knocked on the door of Grandma's bedroom behind the kitchen and called to her. She didn't answer. I knocked harder and called louder, hoping the gnomes wouldn't hear me and be warned. I was certain she must have heard me; I wondered if she knew about the gnomes and was cowering under her pillow in fear.

I raced back along the hall to my bed. I wasn't crying, of course, but my teeth were chattering and I was shivering from the cold. As I pulled the covers up I made myself look out of the window.

It was a clear, moonlit night.

And all the gnomes were in place.

But the noises were still going on. I was still. And I thought. Suddenly I was furious: someone out there was playing a practical joke. No serious burglar would titter like that. No serious burglar would bother to rob my grandmother's house, unless he knew where she kept her money. Maybe that was it. I panicked for a moment, then remembered Mummy and climbed out of bed again, put on my shoes and dressing gown and let myself out of the front door. I did another quick check of the gnomes, but the full complement stood motionless in the moonlight. I stepped off the veranda and waited. There was a slight scuffle and a giggle and I realized the noises were coming from the other side of the fence that separated Grandma's house from the neighbor who had peered through the curtains at me as I arrived the day before.

There were three trees in the side yard. As I ran across to see what was beyond the fence I tripped on a root and thudded heavily to the ground. As I lay there getting my breath back and checking my body to find where the worst breaks were, more noises erupted from behind the fence and over it tumbled three small boys. Not stopping to see how badly injured I might be, they pelted past me down Grandma's backyard and through the gate into the lane.

I stood up, rubbed the gravel from my hands onto my dressing gown, and tottered across to the fence. I must have disturbed them before they'd completed their work, but on the side wall of the house next door the boys had scrawled with white paint, in letters about three feet high: IT! I.T.!

Suddenly I felt the damp chill of the night icing up my veins. It seemed that the silence pulsed around me. The streetlight flickered and dimmed. I hurried back to my bed and the blessed brick that was still warm and comforting.

What sentence did "IT" begin, and why should a group of young boys be painting enigmatic words on the wall of a house in the middle of the night?

Next morning I was surprised to find I had no bruises, but I had forgotten to wind my wristwatch and it had stopped at ten to four—or maybe my fall had jolted it. I could hear noises in the kitchen, so I got up and dressed quickly, not wanting Grandma to think I was lazy as well as being a chatterbox! The old metal alarm clock on the mantel said six thirty-five and Grandma, fully dressed, was setting the table. She was a lot better at it than Grandma Dawson, I'll say that for her. Before I could open my mouth she turned on me.

"Now don't you start again," she said. "I get fed up with you talking all the time. You just remember what I said, seen and not heard, and we'll get on all right. Speak only when spoken to!"

So we sat down to a silent breakfast. But the food was good again. Grandma cut a thick slice of bread, then slipped it onto the end of a toasting fork made of blackened wire. Judging by its odd design she'd bent it into shape herself. Then she opened the front of the stove and toasted it on top of the red ashes. With butter and more of that waxy honey it was the best toast I'd ever had. Then she sliced an enormous green apple across and handed me half on the end of the knife.

"Clean your teeth," she instructed; I gathered she meant by eating the apple. Then she settled her elbows on the table and leaned forward to peer into my face. "Right," she said, "now we'll talk."

I didn't say a word.

"Well?" She glared. "What you want to say, girl?"

I had thought she'd want to ask about my parents, or school, the sort of things adults usually ask, what subjects are you best at, what do you want to be. . . . But all the time I was with her, Grandma never asked that sort of pointless question. So I began to tell her what had gone on the night before. She claimed not to have heard me calling her, a downright lie I was sure.

"I'm one of the world's great sleepers," she boasted, "as soundly as the wretched slave I sleep. Anyway, what were you doing, charging about the place in the middle of the night? Child your age should sleep like the wretched slave too."

There didn't seem enough time to sidetrack after the wretched slave, whoever he—or she—might be, so I forged ahead. "Grandma, there were some boys next door last night, and they painted something on the wall of the house—why the side wall, I wonder?"

"Stands to reason, doesn't it? Good clear space to work on. Too many windows along the front." She licked a honeyed finger. "Well, go on, what did they paint?"

"It," I said.

"It?" I could see that explanations might take more time than we had: "I.T. It. What does it mean, Grandma?"

"How would I know?" But she looked shifty, as if she did know.

"Maybe it's the beginning of a sentence." But to save my life I couldn't have thought of one sentence that started with IT.

"It's a long way to Tipperary," Grandma offered. "It's none of our business." I don't think the latter was an illustration of a sentence beginning with "it" at all. But I intended to find the answer to the riddle.

"Who lives next door? Someone spied on me from there as I arrived yesterday."

"Call themselves Bert and Rose Bell. Yes, she does that a lot. Never goes out. Still." I received the clear message that again it was none of my business. So then I asked when I had to start school and Grandma said I needn't if I didn't want to, at least until after the next lot of holidays. That suited me. I didn't feel like trying to make new school friends as well as coping with a month of Grandma Tucker! Besides, I'd be back in Sydney by next term. So that was a gain.

I was dying to ask why she lived so poorly, what all those gnomes were doing in the front yard, so many questions, but she made me nervous glaring at me as she did. So I asked why she'd laughed when I'd told her I'd had a malted milk at the White Rose Café. Silly question, but it had been puzzling me.

"Did I laugh?" she laughed. "Always strikes me as funny. The White Rose of Rome!"

"It's the white rose of Athens, Grandma, not Rome."

But our colloquy was over. She stood up and pulled a brightly striped beanie over her head. "Well, that's it for now. I must be off. Be back in time for dinner." She hadn't told me she was going out, but there she went out the back door. I followed and asked where she was going. She didn't reply but went to the shed in the back garden, wheeled out an old bicycle and set off around the side of the house.

I cleared and washed the dishes, feeling as miserable as I could possibly be, then I decided to do something about it. I'd telephone Grandmother Dawson right away and tell her I *had* to go back to Sydney or I'd end up as potty as Grandmother Tucker.

I searched every room. There was no telephone in

58

the house! And no wireless! But Grandmother Dawson had told me she had telephoned to say I was coming. . . . No wireless! In fact, there was really nothing that was comfortable or up-to-date in the whole house. Even the sofa and chairs in the front room were hard and unused. I opened the front door. All those gnomes! For something to do I counted them: twenty-four on one side of the path, twenty-five on the other. Forty-nine stupid garden gnomes, each about eighteen inches tall and all in need of a touch of paint!

I strolled to the trees at the side and found the root that had brought about my downfall on the previous night. Since I was so close, I naturally looked over the fence. There on her knees beside the wall was a small, dark woman. Black hair was pulled back from her face by a black bandeau, everything she wore was black and she was scrubbing hard at the painted letters with what smelled like a turpentine-soaked cloth.

"Hello," I said, "I saw them do that, you know. Three boys, in the night."

Her head came round as if it had been slowly pulled by a string. Terrified brown eyes stared at me for a moment, then she scrambled to her feet and tore off toward the back door of her house. She'd left the cloth, and a bottle beside it. I climbed the fence. After my buffeting of the night before I was pleased I could manage the feat. Then I scrubbed hard with the cloth until the two letters turned into a faint smear on the darker paint of the wall.

I corked the bottle and took it and the cloth around the back of the house and knocked on the door. I knocked and knocked. Finally from within the house a timid voice whispered, "See!"

But there was nothing to see but a closed door. I

knocked again, louder, and the door opened a fraction. I shoved the bottle quickly into the opening. It was grasped by an invisible hand. The rag disappeared the same way.

"Mrs. Bell, may I speak to you?" I really was being extremely polite. "Mrs. Bell, what does I.T. mean? Are you all right?"

All I got in reply was another strangled "See!" The woman was obviously crazy. A fitting neighbor for my crazy grandmother. I gave up and climbed back over the fence.

I made a decision at that moment. I would do as Grandma said, mind my own business and go back to Sydney as soon as I possibly could. To this end I went to my bedroom, collected my brown leather handbag and set off down the street to find a telephone so that I might ring Grandma Dawson. I left the front door unlocked too. If Grandma wanted to encourage thieves then that was her problem, not mine. I rather hoped a band of them would come while I was out and find her wretched hoard of money, wherever it might be.

The post office was on the next corner of the main street and when I asked at the counter they directed me to the side of the building and a separate room where an enormously fat lady sat at a switchboard. She was wearing earphones and an enthralled expression on her face. She was so intent on the conversation in progress that she didn't notice me for a while, and when she finally did glance round she lifted a finger to shush me, then pointed with the same finger to a chair beside her. I sat and waited until she had heard enough, then she nodded in a satisfied way and unplugged the wires.

"They've made a wise decision. Cuppa?" Before I could answer she had fished in the basket beside her chair, had the lid of a vacuum flask filled with brackish tea for me and was filling another cup for herself. She ladled four spoonsful of sugar into hers and handed me the jar and spoon. I had decided to say no to the tea, but she was extremely swift for such a beamy lady. (I've noticed that fat people sometimes are extremely nimble.) She had to answer the phones from time to time, by shoving a plug into a hole and trilling "Exchange" into the mouthpiece. Between calls she managed to prize the lid off a big red cake tin.

It was not the happiest day of my life, and the tea and cakes offered by the lady telephonist were a great comfort. She seemed friendly and I could tell she took a deep interest in the affairs of her callers. She was also a dedicated eater; the level of the contents of the cake tin went down rapidly, but I suspected she had another full one for her lunch. Small cakes disappeared as if spirited away by a magic force. One minute a morsel would be held in her immense paw, the paw would pass across the front of her face, and lo! Empty paw, jaws not moving, a smiling face as if nothing had happened in the way of mastication. In a lull between calls she questioned me.

"So you're the grandchild, then. I'm Nell Carter. How's your granny in Sydney, then? My word, she was worried about you. I said it'd be all right for you to come, though. You settling in all right then, love?"

I said no, I wasn't and could she please put a call in for me for the Dawsons' number, which I didn't happen to know because I'd never telephoned them. She had a Sydney telephone directory on top of her switchboard, so she gave it to me and I looked up the number myself.

"Not settling in? Oh well, it's early days yet, isn't it?"

61

She fiddled with the board and found that the Dawsons' number was not answering.

"Not home, love. Anywhere else I can try?"

Grandpa would be at the bowling club and Grandma might be anywhere at all. I shook my head.

"Hey, come on, cheer up. Homesick, are you? Not surprised. It's to be expected. You're a long way from your mum and dad from what I hear. Still, you must admit your granny here's a good old stick."

I decided to question Miss Nell Carter, but subtly.

"Why hasn't my grandmother got the telephone on?"

"Never has had, dear. Lots here don't. But I'll take a message any time. It's no trouble at all. I pop round after my shift and leave a note if they're not in. It's a pleasure."

Further than that she would not go. The subject of Grandma Tucker was one that she didn't want to talk about, except to repeat that she was a good old stick. At each question I asked she found something to jiggle with on her switchboard. So I changed tack and murmured that I hadn't met any of the neighbors yet and was longing to make their acquaintance. What were they like—purely as neighbors, that is, nothing personal required, of course.

"Well, next to your granny there's Mr. Hope and Mr. Miles. Oh, they're very nice gentlemen. The Hopes've been solicitors here for years. That's their office across the road. One of the early settlers, Mr. Charles's grandfather was. Lovely man. Mr. Charles, that is. I didn't know his grandfather of course."

"What about the other side?"

"Yes. Well. Less said about them the better, eh? Let sleeping dogs lie, shall we? Least said soonest mended."

And too many cooks spoil the broth and a stitch in

time saves nine, I could have yelled at the silly woman. Instead I asked her to try the Dawsons' number again, because I wanted to go back to Sydney. She did, and there was again no answer. Why did I have the feeling that she hadn't really tried properly? She could be playing any sort of trick with that metaphysical board she commanded.

So I thanked her for the tea and cakes and picked up my handbag and went home.

As I passed number nine, the mystery house, the curtain twitched again. I recalled the little dark woman inviting me inside to see something but not opening the door to let me in. Why was the less said about them the better, and why would children paint two letters on that house in the middle of the night?

Misery tempted me to retrace my steps to the White Rose Café and buy a chocolate bar, but the thought of facing the somber boy who worked there put me off, so I slouched past the gnomes and spent the rest of the day reading *Three Men in a Boat* by the kitchen fire. It cheered me up a bit and I decided to try to telephone the Dawsons again tomorrow. I might find a more helpful telephonist on duty at the exchange.

As it happened, I decided not to bother. The rotten Japanese shelled Sydney that weekend and the chances of Grandmother Dawson allowing me to come back diminished to nothingness. I was stuck in Parsons Creek whether I liked it or not.

It was late afternoon when Grandma's bike squeaked around the side of the house. I quickly shoved another log into the fireplace and went to the back door to meet her. She was settling the bicycle into its shed.

"Grandma," I called, "why do you have all those gnomes in the front yard?"

She didn't answer me, of course. I'd spoken before I was spoken to. Been heard rather than seen. But she seemed quite cheerful as she bustled inside, and the hot pies she'd brought for our meal were tasty and filling. When we were drinking our tea she said, "Well, now, and how's your father?"

She caught me unawares. I must have chattered on for about twenty minutes while she stared at me and sipped her tea. I could hear myself going on and on and I would have stopped except that somehow I couldn't once I'd begun. I told her about Dad joining up and how Mummy and I had missed him. Finally I said, "I don't know why you don't like them, Grandma. They're perfectly nice people."

"Don't like them? Me?" she shrilled. Then she paused, and in a much quieter voice added: "Like? It's true, of course. Well, as for your mother, I've never set eyes on her, so I can't say I dislike her. But yes, I don't think I like your father very much."

So, she'd admitted it.

"Well, I like him." I could feel red-hot prickles inside my eyeballs.

"That's understandable," she answered. "I haven't seen him for sixteen years. He's probably changed a fair bit by now. Hope so, anyway."

"But he's your son!"

"Ah yes," she said in a brisk tone, "that makes it hard to believe, doesn't it? And sad, I suppose, for you. Still, life seldom turns out the way some of us feel it should. Come now, child, we mustn't sit around here all night chatting."

So we took our bricks to bed and that night, thank goodness, the gnomes were still.

10

Grandma stayed at home on Saturday and together we cleaned the house. I figured she was completely dotty to work so hard when she could well afford not to, and when we came face-to-face in the hallway, me putting on the floor wax, she rubbing it up, I inquired through gritted teeth, "Why do you do this?"

"Keeps me young," she grinned and crawled past me, buffing away at the linoleum like the madwoman she was.

When the house was done we lunched, then washed our cleaning cloths and hung them on the line behind the bicycle shed. As she adjusted the clothes prop I leaned against a big white box and Grandma frightened me witless by bellowing: "Watch out! There's thirty thousand bees in that hive, young lady. You annoy one of them and you'll have a nasty sting or two!"

So that was where the honey came from. She talked quite a lot, for her, about the bees. There was a dish of sugar dissolved in water nearby and the bees got nourishment from that during the winter when their trees weren't blossoming. They lived behind the shed so that their flight path wouldn't lead them near the house. I would have enjoyed seeing Grandma collect the honey, but she said you never rob bees in winter. Poor bees, fancy working all year only to have your honey nicked by someone like Grandma!

"Well, now you've met the bees," she said. "We've got work to do. Come along."

She dragged a large burlap sack from the bicycle shed, rolled it up, tied it around with a piece of string and trudged along the side of the house and out the front gate with me trailing along behind. Very few people were about and all the shops were closed. We went down the main street and turned the corner by the Royal Hotel. Quite a hubbub in there, a wireless crackling horse races and a yeasty smell of beer. I asked where we were going but Grandmother wouldn't tell me, she just stumped along making ploppy sounds with her tennis shoes.

We turned another corner, walked a block or two, crossed a vacant allotment, then stood looking down at the railway track.

"Come on," said Grandma, "but watch your step."

I certainly had to, because the bank was steep and rocky. When we'd both made it to the bottom, Grandma untied the sack and rolled back its opening.

"Should have brought two of these," she muttered. "Still, you can just fetch the light stuff and bring it over to me."

"What light stuff?" I bleated. "There's nothing here, Grandma. It's a railway line. We could be cut in half by a train any minute."

She laughed, delighted. "You know, your father said that too, the first time I brought him here. No trains on Saturday afternoon. Even that bully the station-master takes the day off, so we're quite safe. Just you pick up the small pieces and I'll collect the big ones."

I look around and realized what we'd come for. There was coal on the ground, fallen off the railway trains as they rounded the corner. My grandmother had brought me here, as she had brought my father when he was a child, to steal it for her kitchen fire. Already she was darting about with her bag, picking up and hefting chunks of the black rock to pop into the bag. I sat down on the bank. "I won't do it!" I yelled. "I will not steal!"

She took no notice at all and continued down the track, hopping from sleeper to sleeper, with the red bow in her hair flapping. One blessing was that she wasn't wearing that ridiculous beanie. The enormous tablecloth skirt was swinging from side to side as she moved. Before she disappeared from sight I called again, but again she ignored me, so I stood up, clambered back up the side of the cutting and went home. I didn't feel good about leaving her, and I hoped she could manage to scramble back up the bank with the bag of coal. But she shouldn't be stealing it in the first place and in the second, she obviously stole it all the time, so getting home with the bag of boodle was obviously a problem she'd faced before.

When I arrived at the house I dragged out the compendium that Dad had given me as a present when I left home. It was green leather, stocked with airmail paper and envelopes. There was a special place for stamps, and a fountain pen held in little loops down the center. I wrote a long letter to the Sydney grandparents.

It was difficult to write without telling them how Grandmother Tucker differed from the picture we all seemed to have had of her. Although I longed to confide in them and beg to be called back to Kirribilli, I couldn't bring myself to tell them how she lived . . . what she was doing at that very minute, for instance! So I told them every detail of the trip in the train except the soldier's wink, and how the weather had been compared to Sydney—and indeed compared to weather I'd experienced from time to time in London and every other place I could think of! I enclosed a page and a half for them to send on to my parents. It seemed easier than writing a separate letter and breaking the news of my whereabouts to my mother.

Grandmother arrived home eventually, looking very tired and that made me feel rotten. By the time she came in the front gate the sack of coal was trailing along the ground behind her, dragged by the cord around its neck. I went out to help, thankful that we didn't live right in the main street where witnesses to our crime might be available.

"Got a bit more than usual," she panted. "Thought you'd be there to help me home with it. Decided not to stay, then?"

"Of course I decided not to stay, Grandma! That's stealing! All that coal belongs to the New South Wales Government Railways! You can't just go and take it!"

"Certainly I can," she answered as we lugged the heavy sack around to the bicycle shed. "I just did! I've been taking coal for . . . let me see now, when did I begin?"

I didn't care when her life of crime had started. All I knew was that it had to stop. "Grandma," I shouted, glaring at her across the bundle, "why don't you buy coal? You don't need to steal it. Maybe the station-master . . . I don't know . . . there must be someone who sells fuel . . ."

"Stationmaster? Huh! He won't even permit me to step onto his precious railway station, he won't. Listen, child, the coal falls off the coal tenders. You think the engine driver's going to stop the train and that he and his fireman are going to walk back along the track to pick it up? It's not stealing if something's left lying about. This coal is abandoned. Forsaken. Now let's put some of it on the fire to gyp it up a bit."

After dinner that night, when she permitted talk, I asked her why the stationmaster didn't allow her to set foot on his precious railway station, even when her only grandchild was arriving on one of his trains.

"It's all because of the blessed pigeons."

I waited in case it began to make sense.

"Any pigeons come up on the train with you?"

They had, of course; the crate the young porter had wheeled along on his trolley gave a distinct suggestion of pigeons now that I thought about it.

"They race them," she went on. "Homing pigeons. People—pigeon fanciers—send those big baskets full of poor little birds from Sydney, and Mr. McCann has to open them up, then they fly back to their pigeon lofts in the city and the owners time them and win prizes. The owners win prizes, mind you, not the wretched birds. Those owners don't battle their way up among the big winds and the rain, they just sit at home with their stopwatches in their hands and take the prize if their bird wins. And probably give them no tea if they don't."

"What prizes do they get?" I could perhaps train a few pigeons myself.

"How would I know? Ribbons, I suppose. Well, I used to go down and watch, you see. And one day . . . well, they were so crowded up in there, and I thought an earlier start might give them more daylight to fly in, so I opened the basket. It was a strange thing, they'd looked so glorious when I'd watched Mr. McCann letting them go—they'd billowed out of their box like white balloons, wheeled together and set off for home. But when I did it, they flapped and scratched and clawed and glared at me and fought to be the first out . . . it wasn't a joyous occasion at all, for me or them. They almost took me with them! And Mr. McCann came charging down the platform and ordered me off the place and told me never to come back. I hope the birds got back safely. They don't look as happy up close— anxious eyes, every one of them."

"Well, I imagine they quite enjoy flying, I mean, it's what they do, isn't it? Maybe they like to race. Some people do."

"And maybe they'd like to have the choice of racing or not racing. Ever thought of that?" Grandma grumped.

I went to bed glad that I hadn't helped her steal the stupid coal. But I didn't sleep very well. All the bombers that night had sad staring eyes.

11

Next day after lunch while I cleared away, Grandma put her beanie on, fetched a large pot of honey from the pantry and stowed it in a big canvas bag with handles.

"You ride a bike?" she asked me.

I had, only once, when I was quite small, but I said yes and she wheeled hers out of the shed, hung the canvas bag from the handlebars and pointing to the passenger rack behind the saddle, said: "I do the first bit of pedaling, then it's your turn."

I perched myself on the narrow metal seat, asked where we were going and wasn't answered, then we were off, with me clutching at Grandma's tablecloth, as we wobbled down Park Street. I prayed that no one would see us, but even more strongly I was hoping that a minor earthquake might strike Parsons Creek some time before it was my turn to pedal.

After a block or two we settled into a steady rhythm, my face tingled, the wind lifted my hair, and we'd hardly seen a soul, or, more important, hardly a soul had seen us. Grandma took the road out of town past the silo.

The going was flat and I was beginning to believe that I wouldn't have to pedal the rattling machine after all. But suddenly she stopped, did a few little running steps, and turned a rosy face to mine.

"Thought I wasn't going to let you have a go, didn't you?"

I slid off my perch and we stood there for a while, Grandma holding the bike upright and me rubbing my suddenly throbbingly painful bottom.

"You can't, can you?" she accused.

"Well, I can, but I haven't for a while."

"How long's a while?"

I calculated, "About ten years. I was five."

"Have a go then," she said coldly, giving the handlebars over to me and rescuing her jar of honey just in case.

I squeezed the rubber grips with clammy hands and started off down the road. I was falling . . . no, yes, no. *Mirabile dictu*, it came back to me! As long as I pushed those pedals and leaned rhythmically from side to side, the bicycle stayed upright. When I felt quite confident that I wouldn't topple off I made a classy hand signal, swung the bike around and pedaled back to where Grandma was waiting.

"Good on you," she beamed, "you *can* ride. Mind you, if you'd been lying to me you'd have walked all the way back to town."

I believed her.

With the honey back in the carrier basket and Grandma firmly gripping me around the waist we set off again. She didn't weigh much and I really enjoyed the ride. A couple of miles along the road she directed me into a gap in the fence, we rattled across a cattle ramp and up a drive to a farmhouse. Across another ramp and into the yard, where a small calf lumbered across to greet us, fowls flapped, and three bluish dogs jumped and barked insanely. The door of the house opened and a lady came out wiping floury hands on her apron.

"So this is David's girl," she said. "She's the spit of him too, isn't she, Rachel? How long you staying with us, love?"

"A month," I answered loudly. Grandma was patting one of the dogs and pretended not to hear.

They greeted each other and the lady, Mrs. North, gave me a pillowy hug, Grandma handed over the honey, and we were ushered into the kitchen. There was a black stove, bigger than Grandma's, with huge cast-iron pans gossiping together on top. At the back, beside the chimney, hung a pale mass encased in cloth, dripping steadily but slowly into a dish beneath.

Grandma nodded toward it. "Making more cheese, I see, Mary."

Mrs. North nodded, eased a cat out of her way with the toe of her broad army boot and opened the door of the oven. Out came three vast pies, smelling sweetly of apples.

"One for us, and two for the boys for tea."

Grandma, I was pleased to note, didn't make the ladylike refusals Mummy always did whenever we were invited to eat, but fetched plates down from the dresser instead.

"I'd've made scones, but the apples are so good. Just a sec, I'll get some fresh cream."

Beside the hearth were two shallow steel pans with gauze covers. They were filled with milk. Mrs. North took a big flat spoon and carefully scooped thick clotted cream from the top of one of them to fill a china bowl. We sat at the table and feasted on apple pie and cream and cups of hot sweet tea. Then she sent me to the pantry to fetch cake. A cool Ali Baba's cave it was, full of the most splendid sights and smells. Rows of preserving jars filled with geometrically arranged fruits and vegetables, hams and sausages hanging by strings from the ceiling, even a fat round Christmas pudding swinging in a piece of sheeting, fruit-stained, and giving off sweet, spicy fumes. Strings of onions, a big bag of potatoes, and under a wire-mesh dome, a vast slab of currant cake.

When we finished eating, the two women talked while I wandered through the house. Every door was propped open with an enormous pumpkin, and every room smelled of furniture polish and apples.

I stopped to play with the cat for a while outside the kitchen door and heard Mrs. North say, "I really think you should tell her, Rachel. The child should be told."

"Should?" Grandma's voice was angry. "There's a lot of *shoulds* in there, Mary North."

"I know you don't like the word, Rachel, but you know very well what I mean."

"Yes, old friend, I know. But it's easier if *she* doesn't know. Knowledge brings obligations, and obligations can be a heavy burden."

I dropped the cat, but couldn't rush in to confront them; they'd realize then that I'd eavesdropped, and knowing Grandma, she wouldn't tell me anything anyway. They went on to speak of other things. I sauntered back into the room, seething.

Before we left, Grandma took me down to the orchard, hundreds of apple trees laid out in perfect symmetry and laden with fruit.

"We only take the windfalls," she warned, and we filled her canvas bag from the grass beneath the trees.

74

Then back to farewell Mrs. North, who had a large jar of cream, a square of bright yellow butter wrapped in waxy paper and a large pumpkin to add to our loot.

Going home was harder. With the apples and butter and cream in front and Grandma grappling with the pumpkin behind, it was a mercy we met no traffic on the road. It was almost dark when we came to the town and we had no light, but I had a feeling Grandma wouldn't be bothered by that lack, so I didn't suggest walking the rest of the way.

12

There were so many questions I wanted to ask. Where did Grandma go each day? Where did all those books come from? What was IT? And what did Mrs. North think I should know? Forty-nine garden gnomes was an item I pondered on also. But Grandma just wouldn't answer if I spoke to her outside of her decreed talking times. While she wasn't exactly unkind, she ignored me most of the time, and there was a sternness about her, and an intent stare in her eye, that put me off.

Of course I wasn't lonely. I'm never lonely, but I certainly got a lot of reading done. And one day I found both the "wretched slave" that Grandma slept as soundly as, and the owner of the books! The slave was in *Henry V*, and when I found him I decided that if I were staying longer it might be fun to jot down some of the odd remarks Grandma made and see if I could find what she was talking about in these books. But I wasn't going to stay any longer than I had to. I finished *Henry*, and it made me homesick for England, so I set off for a walk.

Instead of going toward the main street I strolled in

the other direction. And right next door to Grandma's house was the door that was on the bookplates! The house it belonged to was very grand and set well back from the street, with neat lawns and well-tended gardens at the front and sides, a deep veranda with french windows opening onto it . . . and in the middle, there stood The Door! It was made of a glowing dark wood, with a brass knob and the great lion's-head knocker. Long panels of colored glass glowed on it and down the sides.

I stood at the gate and stared, and then a man came around the corner of the veranda. It was the elderly man who'd been on the train with me. The small dog trotted beside him. Before I could move he walked down the path to the gate.

"Good morning, you are Mrs. Tucker's granddaughter, of course. I'm Charles Hope. How do you do?"

I how-do-you-doed him back, and we shook hands.

"I came to check the mailbox." He was making sure I didn't think he'd come to see why I was staring at his house, which I thought was very decent of him. "We have a cup of tea on the side veranda at this time of day, weather permitting, of course. Would you care to join us?"

I did remember Mother's warnings, but this was a neighbor, and quite old, I was dying for something to eat and hoped it wasn't just tea he was offering, and anyway, having found Charles Hope, I was not going to let him go without finding out some more about my odd granny. So I opened the gate, he looked inside the empty letter box, and we walked around the side of the house, with the small dog going quite mad with joy now that he had two more feet to snap at.

In a sunny corner of the side veranda a table was laid

with an embroidered cloth, tea things and a big plate of tiny iced cakes. The other man I remembered was there. His name was Roger Miles. He'd cooked and iced the cakes and we had to be very careful to keep our faces enthusiastic because he was so anxious that we should enjoy them. He was not a very relaxed person, friendly enough, but edgy. They each insisted I call them by their Christian names, so we were Charles, Roger and Kate—and, of course, dog. They just called him dog, and without a capital either, Charles pointed out. He thought it was twee to give animals pet names, but it was Roger's dog and I suspected Roger sometimes called him Diddums when no one was near.

I didn't have to ask questions at first because Roger suddenly asked, "Your father. Is he happy now?"

It was an odd thing to say and Charles looked sharply at his friend as if he'd like him to change the subject.

"That's a funny question," I said, "I really don't know if he's happy or not. He's in the air force."

"An officer, I trust." Roger was waspish and Charles interrupted then.

"Roger and your father didn't quite see eye to eye," he murmured quietly. "But your grandmother is a dear friend of us both, isn't she, Roger?"

"Oh yes, *she* is."

But Roger was another one who definitely didn't care for my father. So I stuck out my chin and asked him why. He smiled very blandly at me and insisted that of course they'd be friends if they met *now* . . . it was years since they'd . . . my father had been a mere child . . .

So I knew he wasn't going to tell me anything more than Grandma had. I turned back to Charles. "Those books in Grandma's house," I inquired, "why do they all have your name inside?"

"Because they belong to him, that's why!" Roger yelped.

Charles laughed. "Forgive my friend. Yes, your grandmother had the books from me."

"Had? You mean she borrowed them?"

"For *him*, of course," Roger interrupted. "She borrowed them for him."

"Very well." Charles took an old bent pipe from his jacket pocket and tapped it against the veranda post until all the old tobacco fell among the plants along the border beneath. Roger watched, horrified as he did it, but said nothing. "She borrowed them so that your father could have books. The school here is small, with no library, and the local lending library is a musty collection of old romances and Sunday School prizes housed in the School of Arts. It's not easy when you have a clever child, eager to learn."

"She could have bought them herself," I suggested. Charles shrugged, stuffing new tobacco into the pipe. "Well, why didn't she return them? My mother says it's stealing not to return books you borrow."

"My books are different," Charles murmured. "There have always been far too many here. Makes for dusting, you know, getting down and moving them about. Your grandmother's always chiding me about having too many movables in this house. Roger's not a keen reader, and my eyesight's not what it was." He stared across the garden with a sad, thoughtful expression in his eyes. "It pleases me that she should have the books. A very small repayment."

"Repayment? What for?" She must have lent him money.

He turned back to me. "What for? For her . . . friendship, I suppose."

Roger cut in. "Friendship? Oh, honestly, Charles,

79

she's always bossing you around. Maybe 'tolerance' is the word you mean."

"I choose to call it friendship, Roger." Charles was angry and Roger lowered his eyes and got busy arranging the cakes that were left on the plate into neat rows.

"I'd call it love," Charles continued, "except that the word may startle this young one. Love's a difficult concept for many people to understand."

"True, Charles, friendship will do."

"Well, I don't think real friends borrow things from you and don't give them back. Grandma should have given the books back." But I wondered how I'd have filled my days if she had.

"My dear child, she wanted to keep them by her. A comfort, some company for her loneliness, words to fill the silences. Would you want her to have to *ask* me if she could keep the books? No, we like to do it this way. It's our pleasure. A sharing."

"I don't mind her having the books," Roger muttered. "She's a great help to me."

The idea of Grandmother Tucker as a kindly benefactor was novel, so I asked Roger what she had done to help him, and was given a jolt that took the wind from my sails. Not that there was much wind left since I'd moved in next door.

What my grandmother did for Roger and Charles was to clean their house twice a week. I managed in a faint voice to ask if she did the same for anyone else in town and was given the answer I should have expected. Grandma worked in other people's houses just about every day of the week. My grandmother was what my mother would call a char!

Roger watched me closely as he spoke. He seemed

to be awaiting some reaction in me. "Are you shocked? Disappointed, disgusted, repelled?" he asked. I was suddenly very angry with him because he seemed to be baiting me. So I conjured up my father's voice again. *Be still.* And I was. *Now think.* And I did.

Grandma must have lost all her money, therefore had to earn some. There wouldn't be many jobs that a woman could do in Parsons Creek.

"No," I answered; I'd hardly had to think about it at all. "I'm not any of those things. I'm just surprised because I didn't know about it, that's all."

Now there (I realized a long time later on) was their chance to tell me something else that I should know, that I really should have been told, but neither of them said a word. They seemed pleased with me though, and when I said I must go, Roger insisted on giving me the rest of the little cakes to take with me, and Charles invited me to come anytime and also to borrow any more books I might like to read. But I was definite in my refusal to do that. Borrow more books, I mean. I had such stacks of them to read already. Anyway, I was only going to be there for a month and I'd never get through that lot in a year. I surprised myself by adding, "Thank you for letting her keep them."

"Don't mention it to her," Charles said as he walked me to the gate. "It's little enough comfort when you consider her loss." I supposed he meant my father going so far away and I silently agreed that it was little enough comfort for that.

That night after dinner I put the plate of cakes on the table and Grandma and I polished off the lot. I told her about my visit next door, skipping lightly over the content of most of the conversation.

"They're very good people," she said. "Roger gets

a bit nervy sometimes. He's always been highly strung, poor man."

Roger didn't seem poor to me and I said so.

"Oh yes he is," Grandma mumbled over a largish bite of cake. "His father had a big property out of here, and expected Roger to stay on and run it. Roger wanted to study music; there were great arguments, I believe. But off he went, his mother helped him, to Sydney to have lessons." She shook her head sadly, and I was afraid she wasn't going to finish the story, but she said: "Turned out he just wasn't good enough. Left it too late, you see. Then his father died and he came rushing back, just in time for his mother to die too. Stupidly, he felt it was his fault. He tried to run the property, but it was too much for him. Made a lot of money when he sold it, but . . . poor man, he's had a sad life. Still, he's a good cook."

But the story still wasn't complete. How about Mr. Hope? Charles?

"Charles is a different kettle of fish altogether. He and Roger were at school together, then Charles went to the war and afterward to university and came back here, a solicitor, like his dad was before him. It was him encouraged David, your father." She didn't continue on that track. "Then, when Roger sold up he was so ill he had to have a spell in hospital, and afterward Charles invited him to move in with him. They've been together ever since. Charles is semiretired now."

"Roger doesn't seem to like Daddy."

She looked at me for a long time and I thought I might have brought conversation to an end for the night, but she went on: "It was difficult for both of them. Charles had been such a help to your father, with books and encouragement. And then David went to university in Sydney, and when he came home Charles was busy helping Roger get over his problems . . . maybe your father felt left out of things . . . I don't know . . . it was a hard time for everyone."

Some explanation!

13

We settled into a reasonably comfortable routine. I was very careful to ask no questions except when Grandma wanted to talk, and while she was out at work I tidied the house, did a bit of schoolwork now and then, read books, sat in the park, and went for walks around the town. So I came to know Parsons Creek well, specially the post office, because I wrote often to my Dawson grandfolk and my parents. I didn't bother trying to telephone again. I figured I could last out the month more easily than I could explain things to Sydney! Also my letters were extremely unspecific because I didn't know yet whether my parents had been told that I'd come to Parsons Creek. I certainly didn't want to be the one to tell them. The war was bad enough, England didn't need Mummy carrying on as I knew she would! So I still enclosed my letters to her and Dad with the ones I posted to the Dawsons and told them all a lot about the state of the weather and what books I was reading, often including a comprehensive outline of the plot.

Grandma Dawson replied to each of my letters in her

crabby little writing on thick creamy paper with deckled edges. She never used airmail paper, so letters to England must have cost her the earth. Her letters told me nothing and she never directly referred to my enclosures, merely said each time, "I've just sent off a letter to your parents, dear." I suppose she didn't want to actually say the letter was mine in case Grandma Tucker read it and got angry or something. Not that she would. I've never met anyone as infuriatingly incurious as Grandma Tucker.

I hadn't asked her about my grandfather at all. I knew we were all terribly proud of him, but I didn't want to start her up grieving again, so I just never mentioned his name.

One day the park looked inviting, the sun was bright enough to cast shadows under the trees, so I took a book across to read on the grass. I had to pass the War Memorial, with the names of the fallen lettered in gold down the side and *Lest We Forget* around the top.

I paused to read the names. There was no Tucker listed!

I looked on each side. There was not one Tucker there. My own grandfather had been killed with the Light Horse at Gallipoli and his name was not on the town honor roll! I vowed to face Grandma that night with a few pertinent questions. As it happened, events made me change my plans—and I must admit it, I was becoming more and more reluctant to ask for details of my father's family. Grandma's lack of curiosity was catching. As well as that, the details I did hear were seldom pleasant!

My plans for the evening changed when I was walking down the main street en route to a malted milk. A voice behind me said "Good day" and someone tapped me on the shoulder. I turned, and there was the soldier who'd come on the train with me. The good-looking one. He was dressed in ordinary clothes but I would have known that Rupert Brooke face anywhere. He was with another boy whom I'd seen in Eldershaw's Emporium. He seemed to be employed there but he never offered to help—he seemed to spend his time creeping around behind the fittings and trying not to look customers in the eye in case he had to serve them. He had a pleasant face when he smiled, which he was doing now, and tightly curling blond hair and dark-brown eyes.

"Name's Jim," the soldier said. "And this here's Tom Eldershaw. Thought you mightn't recognize me in civvies. I'm Parker."

By the time I'd worked that out and told them my name I felt as if I'd known them both for years.

"Seen you around," Tom Eldershaw said. "You're staying with Mrs. Tucker, aren't you? She your granny?"

He talked in such a lively manner that I could scarcely believe he was the same skulker I'd seen in the shop, and I had to concentrate really hard to stop my mouth from widening up into one of my goofy grins. And I was really glad that Jim remembered me. He said he had only ten days' leave and he'd be going back to his army camp in three days so why didn't we do something one of these evenings, eh? Tom joined in again to say that he was going to Sydney to enlist in the air force in five weeks and three days, as soon as he turned eighteen, and what about tonight and the pictures?

Of course I knew that Grandma wouldn't let me go . . . with a serviceman whom I'd met once and a complete stranger! But I'd passed the School of Arts several times and Leslie Howard was on in *Pimpernel Smith*, and I've just adored Leslie Howard ever since I saw him with Mummy in London in *Gone With the Wind*. . . . Because I so much wanted to see the movie I said I'd ask Gran, and I skipped the malted milk and belted off home. I caught her just as she was coming out of the bicycle shed with a load of vegetables, and I took them from her and grabbed the bag and hung there so that she couldn't turn away. I was determined to cling to her and the potatoes until she answered. Fact is, I gabbled so much that she let go of the bag, pushed me off a bit and said, "Now, start all over again. What's the problem?"

And *mirabile dictu*, she didn't raise any of the objections that Mummy or Grandma Dawson would have. If I wanted to go it was quite all right with her. She even offered to lend me one of her tablecloth skirts, obviously having no fondness for any of the clothes I had brought with me.

I washed my hair and sat on the floor in front of the stove with my head practically in the oven to dry it, and wished I'd had the sense to spend some of my money on cosmetics. I'd walked past the chemist shop often enough, but the girl behind the counter had perfect skin and was so gorgeous that I really didn't want to discuss the subject of my face with her at all.

When I was dressed and ready, Grandma came into the bedroom to look me over. "Well," she admitted, "you don't polish up too badly, I'll say that for you." The first compliment she'd ever paid me! Then the front gate squeaked, the brass gnome gonged and the boys arrived. Tom and Grandma must have been old friends because he gave her a big hug and told her about his enlisting, but that didn't please her at all.

"You know my feelings about wars, Tom Eldershaw. I thought you'd have had more sense. I can understand *him* wanting to go"—nodding a disdainful head at Jim— "he's never been too bright. But you! Wars only benefit the people who make the guns."

Both boys looked sheepish. Then we set off and Grandma didn't offer me any advice, or ask what time I'd be home, or tell me to be careful. I felt quite grown-up all of a sudden.

We collected Jim's girlfriend on the way. Helen. I hadn't seen her since the day I arrived at the railway station. Hadn't admired her very much then, but although she giggled a lot she was quite fun. When we went inside the School of Arts hall Jim was loudly disappointed to find all the back row of seats taken, but we settled about halfway down on the aisle. A few minutes later we had to stand up for "God Save the King." There was a piano at the side of the stage, played by a lady in a long blue dress, with gold corrugated hair. An elderly couple near us joined in with the words. I would have liked to as well, but I didn't want to embarrass the boys.

A Movietone Newsreel was on first, and we all clapped when it finished the war news. Then we watched a comedy called *The Smiling Ghost*. It was very juvenile, but scary in parts, so Tom slid his hand across to hold mine. I don't know why people do that. Both of our hands were hot and damp in no time at all, and after a while my arm went to sleep. The whole thing was most uncomfortable, so as soon as the lights came on at intermission I reclaimed my suffering limb and began to wonder what I could possibly do to avoid contact in the second half.

A boy came shuffling down the aisle with a tray hanging from a strap around his neck. "Peanuts, lollies and chocolates," he muttered in a supremely disinterested voice, as if he didn't want anyone to know he was there. I looked at him more closely. Sure enough, it was the boy from the White Rose Café. I quickly turned away, but Tom called out in a loud tone, "Hey, Roberto! Come on over here, will you?"

He came, glaring, and the boys took a long time choosing chocolates for us. They seemed deliberately slow about it and after he'd gone Jim said, "Damn Eyetie. Should be in an internment camp."

"Oh, I dunno." Helen was much less critical, I suspect, because of the shortage of young men in town. Jim was returning to camp in three days. "Roberto was in our class at school. He's all right."

"Oh sure. He was all right at school. But we weren't fighting them then, were we? Mind you, my uncle's in Libya and he reckons Italians make pretty pathetic soldiers."

Helen tried to shush the boys, but Tom had something to add. "Old man Bellini rushed back to enlist with Mussolini as soon as the war started, didn't he? I reckon it's pretty rough having to put up with people like that in town, with a war on and all that."

Roberto was hardly five rows away from us and I knew he could hear every word, and was meant to. But it wasn't my business to try to change their minds about the Italians, and anyway, I felt very much the same myself. He looked big and tough enough to fight his own battles. I had sufficient troubles of my own. As soon as the lights went down again I had to keep fossicking among the chocolates so that my poor hand would be left alone, or remember to keep my arms securely folded. Despite my preoccupation with such maneuvers I enjoyed the film tremendously.

It was cold and rainy when we came out. Jim and

Helen hurried off together and Tom and I had to dash from awning to awning for shelter. When we arrived at Grandma's front door we were both damp and out of breath.

"Good night then," Tom whispered. He put his hands on my shoulders and turned me toward him. I leaned sideways just a little, but enough. The door swung open and we had to stumble apart.

"Good night, Tom. Thank you for a very pleasant evening," I said as I drifted inside.

There was no sign of Grandma. She didn't even bother to wait up for me. An indication of how much she cared about her grandchild's welfare! At the same time, it was a relief to be able to go to bed without the third-degree interrogation that Mummy and Grandmother Dawson liked to administer whenever I went out, even in broad daylight.

Next morning at breakfast, Grandma asked if I'd enjoyed the outing. I said I had.

"This town suit you then?" she asked.

I thought before I answered. I certainly didn't want to give the impression that Parsons Creek would suit me forever, but it was turning out to be a reasonable sort of town. So I told her that it wasn't too bad, and that the boys and Helen were good company.

"Your father liked it too. When he was your age."

"He never talks about it, Grandma."

"No. I didn't think he would. Well, I must be off."

And off she went, leaving me to puzzle about my father.

14

I think there's something wrong with my digestive system, because there are times when I must have sugar and lots of it, otherwise I begin to feel quite wan. I had an attack of this malady the day after we'd been to the cinema. I developed a really painful craving for a milk shake. So I walked down to the White Rose. Roberto was there, as gloomy as ever. I remembered to order a malted straightaway this time, and as I was the only customer I decided to make him talk to me for a while.

"I saw you at the pictures last night, Roberto."

"Name's Bell. Bert Bell."

My first reaction was to laugh because he was the most unlikely Bert Bell you could imagine, then I remembered. Bert Bell! Grandma's next door neighbor, although I'd never seen him in Park Street. The boys had seemed to know him well . . . they'd called him Roberto, and his father "old man Bellini." Roberto Bellini. An Italian name if ever I'd heard one. I remembered Grandma laughing at the White Rose of Rome. So I raised my eyebrows as far as they'd go.

"Bert Bell! How can you call yourself Bert Bell when

you've a simply marvelous name like Roberto Bellini?"

"Yeah. Aren't I lucky," he sneered. "What's your name? Elizabeth? Margaret Rose? Like one of your princesses?"

"Katharine," I said as I came out of the glass for air, "like one of our queens actually. Catherine of Aragon. I'm Katharine Tucker."

"Bravo," he sneered again, "with a name like that they're not likely to run you out of town then. Bet your daddy's fighting on the right side too."

I was really angry with him now. "He certainly is. He's in the Royal Air Force. A Spitfire pilot, that's all. And he's shot down I don't know how many Germans. Italians too, I'm sure."

He stepped back in mock awe. "You mean your daddy's a hero? Shot down all those dirty huns and cowardly Eyeties? Boy, are you lucky."

"I'm not lucky at all." I could have cried I was so angry. "He is a hero. He's already got the DSO and the DFC, if you know what that means. And I am not lucky, stuck away here . . ."

He leaned forward then and poured an extra scoop of malt into my glass, then stirred it absentmindedly with my spoon.

"I don't want any more of that stuff," I yodeled, but I grabbed the spoon and licked it anyway. Sometimes I have no self-control at all.

"Okay, okay," he hissed, "so I won't charge you for it. And I've heard about your famous father, too, so don't bother telling me any more about him."

"What do you know about my father?"

"Not much. But my mother, she reckons he's not half the man your granny is. I'm sorry I can't stand here discussing our fathers' bravery or otherwise. I just cleaned up the glass and I'm now going to put the mop and stuff away, ready for tomorrow. Right?"

"Right! Put the mop away! What's so great about that? Nobody *makes* you clean your windows every day. So why grumble?"

"Oh no. Nobody makes me. Except some kids come around every night with chalks and whitewash and scribble messages on it, don't they? You expect me to leave that sort of thing on the glass all day for people to see? For my mother to see?"

"Well, I'm sorry about your mother, but you can hardly blame them, can you? I mean, I've heard your father did go back to Italy to join up and fight on their side. I mean, I can understand how the people in town must feel." Now I could understand something else too, the paint on the wall of the Bellinis' house. IT for "Italians."

He looked at me for a long time without saying a word. I finished my malted milk. As I pushed the glass across the high counter he said in a very quiet voice, "You can understand, can you? Congratulations. Well, let me tell you something, Queen Katharine Tucker. *You're* not half the man your granny is, either."

He took my glass and walked toward the back of the shop and I slunk out the door. If I'd had a can of whitewash on me at that moment I swear I'd have painted something *really* insulting right along the front of his shop.

That night, when Grandma decided we would talk, I told her about Roberto.

"What's he got to be so crabby about? He should be grateful he's allowed to live here, with his father fighting on the other side. He should be glad he's not interned."

"Ah," said Grandma, "he should, should he? Should,

93

should, should. There's always someone knows how everyone else *should* behave."

"Well, there's a war on. He should . . ."

"Has it ever occurred to you, my girl, that *that* might just be one of the real reasons there *is* a war on? Because someone wants to tell someone else what he should be doing? Take that Hitler chap. He's a great one for bossing people about. There's a lot to be said for letting people get on with things without interference, you know, Kate Tucker. Most folks muddle along pretty well in their own way. And that goes for countries too! I don't hold with wars." No maps with colored pins on her walls!

She hadn't finished. "You think you know how Roberto should feel and act? How anyone should feel and act? What presumption! You want other people to tell you how *you* should feel and act?"

She was right, of course, but it took me a while to admit it. When I did and said I was sorry and felt ashamed of myself she absolutely glowed with pleasure and leaned across the table to pat my hand. But I still thought Roberto was a pain.

"He said his mother knew Daddy. Why doesn't she like him? What did he ever do to her?"

Grandma stood up. "He's wrong. The Bellinis came after your father went to Sydney. There's too much gossip in this town. Far too much. It comes of people spending too much of their time talking, that's the trouble."

And being reminded of how much she disliked the practice of talking, she stopped abruptly and marched off to bed.

15

When Grandma was at home we usually sat in the kitchen, each reading a book. She'd read all the ones in my bedroom and was into *War and Peace* again, her third try. She said she'd been scared off by all the names the first time, the second time she'd skipped the war bits, but now she was going for the lot, and was already well into the second volume. I enjoyed the books, but I did miss the wireless, and one night I decided to do something about it.

A decision I was to regret bitterly.

I started off by asking Grandma, when talking was permitted, why she didn't have a set.

"What would I want with a wireless?" she said crankily. "I've no time to be sitting about listening to all that noise."

But I knew the real reason was that her miserliness wouldn't allow her to spend the money on buying one. So the next time I was in the main street I went into the general store. There was no sign of Tom; he must have found a really effective place to hide from the customers. Mr. Eldershaw senior had ladies working in every department of his shop, but I don't think he really trusted them to sell, because everywhere you turned there he was himself, smiling and nodding his shiny bald head and lifting his eyebrows, trying to entice you to say something flattering about his goods.

I'd been in the Emporium the week before with Grandma. She'd planned to buy a tablecloth, perhaps with another skirt in mind. She paid no attention at all to poor Mr. Eldershaw, who bobbed about her like a moth at a light globe from the moment she walked in the door.

Finally he elbowed the saleslady out of the way and started showing her tablecloths himself. He had boxes of them and Grandma fingered every one and rejected them all. Mr. Eldershaw didn't seem to mind not having made a sale, and as he carefully folded the cloths and layered them back in their boxes he smiled sweetly at Grandma and said, "And how are you keeping, Rachel? Haven't seen you for weeks." He sounded as if he'd really missed her.

"I've been very well, thank you, Paul," she answered in her brisk way. She turned aside to peer speculatively at a really hideous checked blanket that I was positive no one could wear. But clothes rationing had just begun, so Grandma's ideas of tablecloth skirts and blanket wear weren't bad in theory.

Then Mr. Eldershaw said, "My offer still stands, you know, Rachel. Still stands."

But Grandma didn't answer. I wondered what his offer was. Maybe he wanted her to come and work in the store for him. I doubted Grandma would encourage many people to buy. She didn't smile and nod at people at all, and never talked if she could help it.

Obviously Mr. Eldershaw hadn't taken the rebuff to

heart. Today he popped up beaming all the way to his eyebrows and scalp and asked how I was and how Grandma was, and could he help me. He had in stock a dear little wireless that was marked "A Sacrifice at £5/10/-." It was made of brown Bakelite that looked just like walnut and it even had a shortwave band. Mr. Eldershaw plugged it in to show me how it worked and while we waited for it to warm up I fished from my handbag the envelope that Grandmother Dawson had given me. There were five one-pound notes in it, every one crisp and new, just as you'd expect her money to look. With ten shillings of the five pounds that Grandpa had given me for spending I'd be right to pay for the wireless. Just as well, because there was a big sign on the wall that said "Please do not ask for credit, as refusal may offend."

Finally the little machine ceased to crackle and whistle and I watched carefully as Mr. Eldershaw demonstrated how it worked. When I told him I was buying it as a present for Grandma he beamed even harder than usual and insisted on giving it to me for five pounds even.

"Your grandmother's a fine woman, my dear, a fine woman, fine woman." When I told him it was to be a surprise he beamed wider still. "She'll be delighted, delighted. Yes, delighted."

I doubted whether delight was an emotion that Grandma knew much about, but I hoped he was right. He carried the box to the door of the shop for me, then waved me off, calling after me, "Tell Rach—Mrs. Tucker I said good day. Don't forget now, don't forget."

So that night after dinner I told her he'd said good-day.

"What did he say that for?" she wondered; fortunately she didn't inquire what I was doing in the shop!

"I think he likes you, Grandma," I told her, and then she pulled down the sides of her mouth and cocked her head to one side. "He maybe does," she said. "Gave me a wondrous gift of paint once. So many colors!"

"Is that . . . ?" I nodded toward the front of the house.

"Yes. I had the fun of Cork doing those bricks, took me hours to decide which color went beside which. They're sadly due for another go now, but I suppose it's too much to hope he'll have another flood." To my startled look she answered: "Yes, we had a flood here, about ten years ago. Three foot six right through the main street, so of course Eldershaw's basement was underwater. Labels washed off just about everything. My word, that shop was a mess. We all helped clean up afterward, of course, and Paul gave me a present of all those tins of paint. I tell you, young Kate, it was one of the most exciting times of my life, opening them all up and taking a bit of this and a bit of that to do those bricks. And the gnomes."

It was the first time she'd mentioned those gnomes since I'd arrived, and as she stood up to begin clearing the table I grabbed the chance to find out more.

"Grandma," I said, "why do you have all those gnomes out there?"

But she answered not a word.

16

I decided that an occasion must be made of Grandmother Tucker Receiving Her First Wireless. She didn't have much fun in her life, it seemed to me. Going out to work in other people's houses every day and sometimes Saturdays as well, and not even a bit of music to cheer things up. So I planned a little surprise party for her for the following night. I popped in next door as soon as she left on her bicycle. Roger answered the door and showed me into a most elegant sitting room. There was a log fire in the grate and the room smelled of lavender polish and sparkled with glass and china ornaments. Jeweled Persian rugs lay on the polished floor. Roger watched as I looked around, and smiled proudly. "My decorating skills and your dear grandma's elbow grease. Charming, isn't it?"

It was. Charles wasn't home and that was a disappointment, because I would have appreciated his advice about the party. As things turned out, it was an outright calamity he wasn't there to advise me. But Roger was willing to help. He was delighted with the idea.

"My dear, I love parties." He beamed. "Would you like me to bring my violin? No, of course not. Not a good idea at all. No. But I tell you what. I insist on bringing some of my petits fours. Now, how many are we having?"

Of course I had no idea. Charles and Roger were the only friends of Grandma that I'd met, except for Mrs. North at the farm, and I had no way of getting in touch with her. I had hoped that Roger would advise me whom to invite, but then his enthusiasm seemed to wane a bit and he pretended not to know the names of Grandma's friends himself.

"A surprise party," he murmured. "Hmmm. I wonder if we really should? Better not make too much fuss. She can be tetchy, you know. She's been a tad scotty with me from time to time, for no reason at all. Perhaps we shouldn't . . . you're sure you want this? A surprise? You're sure?"

I assured him that I did want it, I was sure, so he suggested the Bellinis. My only encounter with Mrs. Bellini had been less than satisfactory and I didn't fancy an evening of argument with her son either, but Roger assured me that my grandmother was particularly fond of the Bellinis, and it would be such a treat for Rosa, who scarcely ever left the house.

"Just the six of us, I think, dear. Any more and you've got a strain on the plate and cup situation. We could bring in ours, of course, but I doubt if your gran . . . Oh, I really don't know. You do insist on this party idea now?"

I did insist and left him dithering about what colors to ice his petits fours while I summoned up courage to knock on the Bellinis' door.

I knocked and knocked and finally a small voice

whispered "Who?" from right behind it. "Who" and "see" were the only words I'd heard Mrs. Bellini utter. Of course now I knew she was Italian, the "see" made more sense. I explained who I was and the door opened a fraction and a large brown eye peered out at me. It seemed a friendly eye, but its owner had said hurtful things about my father, and I rather hoped she was a conscientious objector to parties. She said nothing until I had finished my speech, and seemed to have the idea that Grandma had sent me. But then she opened the door a little more and added a wide mouth and a shy smile to the eyes I'd already met. She spoke English quite well, for an Italian, and thanked me warmly.

"Such good for Roberto. Eight o'clock tomorrow evening. We come." And then, as I was walking down the path she called, "Hey! I good cook. You tell your nonna I bring lasagne, eh?"

So it was my turn to thank her, and believe me I was mightily relieved. I was certainly no good cook myself. I'd never planned a party before and I hadn't thought what I was going to give them to eat.

Rosa called out again: "Hey!" I turned. "You sure your nonna want people to come?"

I assured her that I was sure my nonna wanted people to come, because it seemed easier than explaining that my nonna didn't so far know anything about it, and that was the whole idea of a surprise party.

The next day I went to the general store and scouted around among the groceries. We were already set for petits fours and lasagne, whatever that might turn out to be. I'd never had Italian food. But I spotted the Sao biscuits and the problem was solved.

. . .

That evening the meal seemed to take longer than usual. I hoped Grandma would have enough room left for some of Roger's little cakes. I knew I would. There was also a chance that she might decide to have a really early night, so as we drank our tea I decided to spill some of the beans in an effort to keep her up.

"I met Mrs. Bellini today," I said.

Grandma was surprised, and not without cause, since everyone seemed to believe that Mrs. Bellini was nailed to the floor of her house.

"She looked out as I went past," I lied. "And she asked if it'd be all right if she popped in to see you tonight. About eight."

"Ah, the poor girl might need something. She never leaves the house. I'll drop over when we've washed up. Save her the trouble."

"No! No, Grandma. She wants to come here. She said so. She does not want you to go there."

"Why not? I've been there often. In and out for years."

"Ah. Yes, well, it's Roberto. Must be a secret. I really had trouble understanding everything she said, but she did say, please wait here until she comes."

Nothing mystified Grandma too much. She just nodded. "Well, if that's what she wants." She showed no curiosity at all concerning the astonishing change in Mrs. Bellini's habits.

By now it was twenty to eight, and there were Saos to be fixed. On the pretext of fetching another book I went to my room. Hidden under the bed beside the wireless was the packet of biscuits, a slab of cheese and some butter I'd stolen from Grandma's meat safe, a knife and a plate. I spread my towel on the bed and buttered and cheesed the big squares. Then I remembered that the great feature of the Dawson Saos and cheese was that Grandmother D toasted them under the griller of the belligerent gas stove. But Grandma T's kitchen lacked both a gas stove and a griller. I decided that when suppertime came I'd stick the plate in the oven and hope for the best.

17

It was almost eight o'clock. My stomach was lurching and my palms were damp with sweat. I nipped back to the kitchen and there was Grandma, intent upon *War and Peace* at the table. She'd changed into her old pom-pommed slippers and I wondered if I could persuade her to tart up a bit for the visitors. But that would let the secret out, and actually Grandma "tarted up" was very little different from Grandma untarted. In fact, the slippers were a trifle more gala than the white tennis shoes she habitually wore. So I didn't say anything and just as well, because there was a thumping at the front door and all the guests came down the hall together.

Mrs. Bellini arrived at the kitchen door first and rushed across to kiss Grandma on each cheek. Grandma was surprised. I suppose she thought that Mrs. Bellini, having a problem to discuss, would look less joyful. Then came Roberto, grim as usual, bearing a large baking pan that smelled delicious. When Grandma saw him, she looked even more nonplussed, and Charles's and Roger's entrance left her utterly slack-jawed.

"Surprise, Grandma!" I yelled, "it's a surprise party!"

She was staring anxiously from one guest to another

and not looking cheerful at all. Neither did Charles, who came forward and took her hands in his.

"Rachel, dear," he murmured, "I only heard about this a few minutes ago. Can you manage?" She nodded mutely and I threw in another "Surprise!" together with a nervous whinny. Roger, who'd been hovering in the hallway, came forward then and gave me some much appreciated support. He hugged Grandma and waved his cake tin in front of her face.

"It's a party, dear. I've brought my petits fours, specially for you."

"Thank you, Roger," Grandma answered gravely. "I'll make some tea."

Something seemed to be horribly wrong and I had no idea what it was. They were all very ill at ease and even Roberto didn't bother to argue with me. He just sat beside his mother and gloomed. She sliced up the lasagne she'd brought and we all had some. It really was the tastiest dish I'd had ever. All tomatoey and rich. Charles told us about his trip to the city, where he'd heard about a really old man who'd dyed his hair and tried to enlist because he believed they weren't doing things right in the army and he knew he could finish off the war for them. Probably Grandpa Dawson.

Roger's petits fours came on and as I bit into one I said, "Tell me about the garden gnomes. What *are* they doing in the front garden?"

It was the sort of remark I'd heard my mother make thousands of times to visitors, well not about gnomes exactly, but just a lighthearted inquiry that most people seem to enjoy answering at parties. This party was different. They all looked extremely uncomfortable. No one said a word, until Charles leaned forward to smile at Grandma.

"Rachel," he said, "we haven't remembered the story

105

of Jack for years, have we? Why don't we tell Kate about him?"

Grandma's somber face crinkled into a big laugh. "The Jaunting Gnome," she chortled. "Of course. Do you know, Charles, I'd completely forgotten about him. You tell her."

We all settled down to listen, me with special attention because I had feared this party would go down in history as the very worst ever.

It seemed that years ago, the local mayor, who was also the bank manager, was a particularly obnoxious man and he'd stolen a gnome from Grandma's collection. I didn't ask the question that at once occurred to me, why would anyone want to steal a *gnome*? It seemed wiser not to interrupt now that someone was talking at last.

He'd put the stolen gnome in his back garden, and to punish him Charles and Grandma had sneaked in one night when he was out, taken the gnome away and hidden it in Charles's house. Some people Charles knew were going to Europe at the time, so he and Grandma composed lots of messages and whenever their ship came into a port they bought a postcard and sent one of the messages back addressed to the mayor, signed "Jack the Garden Gnome." Since the postcards came with no envelope they were read by the postmistress and the postman, who told everyone in town that the mayor was getting postcards from a gnome. And not only that, from a gnome who claimed to have run away from home because of ill treatment at the hands of the mayor—beatings and starvation, no less! The editor of the local newspaper even ran a story each time a postcard arrived, telling the townsfolk the whereabouts of Jack the Jaunting Gnome and the adventures he was having.

By the time Charles's friends had added some local incidents to the postcards, Jack was having a hilarious time and the poor mayor was too embarrassed to show his face except when he absolutely had to. He tried to bribe the postmistress, who of course refused to tamper with His Majesty's mails. The postman denied having even mentioned the content of the postcards to a soul, and the newspaper editor looked blank and said, "What postcards? My stories are fiction. Whoever heard of a small concrete garden gnome taking a sea trip, writing postcards!"

The whole town sided with the cruelly-done-by gnome, who took to including pathetic little messages of forgiveness in his missives. By the time the voyagers had completed their tour it was obvious that the mayor had suffered enough, so Jack the Jaunting Gnome came home! One morning he appeared back in the mayor's garden, the front garden this time, firmly cemented in by the front door, with a tiny suitcase gripped in his little hand, and sporting a glowing suntan from his last stop in Singapore. By coincidence, most of the town's inhabitants just happened to be passing the mayor's house that day. All of them commented on how well the little chap looked after his holiday, and hoped that he and the mayor would be able to settle their differences now. Soon after, the mayor/bank manager was transferred to another branch of that particular bank.

"Jack the Jaunter was never seen again," Charles chuckled. "I think he was probably chewed up into small pieces and spat out."

I enjoyed the story and liked the idea of Charles and Grandma playing a joke together, but after it was told the party went silent again. So I stood up.

"Now all stay where you are," I announced. "I have a surprise gift for Grandma, won't be long." And I sped

107

into my bedroom. There on the dressing table was the plate of biscuits and cheese. I'd quite forgotten about them, but I left them there and hauled the wireless out from under the bed. I carried it to the kitchen, placed it with some ceremony on the sideboard and plugged it into the wall socket. Then I switched it on and turned to lead the applause and see the pleased surprise on Grandma's face. It wasn't there, there was no applause. It was as if I'd brought a tiger into the room. It was too late for me to ask what was wrong, because by now the crackling noises were fading and the announcer was in the middle of a news bulletin.

Everyone stared at me with what looked like loathing, and I stared at each of them in turn, wondering what on earth I'd done, waiting for someone to smile. No one did, and when the stupid announcer said that the battle in Libya had reached a climax, with heavy loss of Italian troops on the southern flank at El Alamein, Mrs. Bellini uttered an ear-cracking shriek, flung her head down on the table and sobbed loudly.

Charles stood up and strode over to the wireless. "Switch this thing off, please, Katharine," he said in a very stern voice.

Roger stood up too. "Well, we'll be off now, dear," he said to Grandma. "Thank you for a lovely party." And they both walked out.

Roberto gathered up his still wailing mother, gave me the look I was becoming accustomed to, of venomous dislike, and led her out of the room. As he passed me he muttered, "You've a great sense of humor, Katharine Tucker."

That left Grandma, who was still sitting at the table, looking tiny and forlorn. I sat down opposite her.

"Grandma, tell me what I did wrong." I longed to follow Mrs. Bellini's example.

"Wrong? You did nothing wrong, Kate. I didn't tell you. How could you have known."

But suddenly I did know. Why Grandma liked children to be seen and not heard, why she had no telephone or wireless set, and why she didn't enjoy surprise parties.

Then I did put my head down on the table and bawl.

18

"I am sorry," said Charles. "I would have told you if I'd known what you planned, my dear."

"Didn't you know she lip-reads?" Roger asked me. "I thought you knew she was deaf." I suspected him of helping me to arrange the party as a prank, and I think the same possibility occurred to Charles, because he said, "Roger, would you mind if I talk to Katharine alone for a moment?" and Roger left the room in a sulk.

It was the morning after my disastrous party. Grandma had pedaled off to work at her usual time. We'd hardly spoken at breakfast, because all of a sudden I felt embarrassed and reluctant to disturb her silences, and I could think of nothing to say that wouldn't reduce me to a howling heap again. I'd woken up with hot eyes and lips like sausages.

I was mooching about among the gnomes when Charles called out and invited me in for morning tea. My first reaction was to run away and hide rather than face his wrath, but then I was still for a moment, and thought, and decided there was nothing he could say or do that would make me feel worse than I already did. At the back of the despair was also a tiny glimmer of resentment that no one had told me Grandma was deaf, so I marched next door in the hope that at last I might learn something of the truth about my peculiar relative.

When Roger had gone, Charles poured me more tea. "I shan't offer you another of Roger's secret weapons," he grinned. "I think he and the local dentist are fifth columnists, out to ruin our teeth. Worth looking after yours—you're going to be a beauty in a year or two, you know." I didn't know, but appreciated the kind words.

"Now, about your grandmother. I presume you wish to talk about it?" I nodded, wishing he hadn't mentioned the beauty thing, because another petit four would have been a comfort at that moment.

"She's been profoundly deaf for about ten years," he said. "She lip-reads very well, but of course she has to be looking at you as you speak to know what you're saying."

So that was why I'd had so many questions unanswered! Grandma had been facing the other way when I'd spoken to her!

"She's managed so well that a lot of people in town don't even know that she can't hear them. She claims she's not missing much! Her friends all know, of course, but we feel it's her business. If she doesn't want others to know, we won't say anything."

"Wish you'd told me."

He patted my hand. "My dear. I'm really sorry. It would have saved you some anguish, I know that now, but believe me, we tend to forget about it most of the time, because your grandmother makes light of it, you see. She doesn't treat it as a tragedy. A nuisance per-

111

haps, but not something she wants people to pity her for, and she wouldn't have told you, because she feels so strongly about family obligations. That there shouldn't be any, I mean."

He talked to me for a long time and I felt much better for it. The deafness came after my father went to England. Grandma never told him about it because she didn't want him to worry about her.

"Wrong decision, I think," Charles commented. "David should have had to face up to things, but his mother would dispute that. She doesn't feel anyone should *have* to do anything just because of family ties. Shouldn't be told to, anyway. That's her main objection to Hitler, you know. He's bossy!"

I told him she had made that point to me, and we paused for a laugh about it. Well, he laughed. I managed a dim smile.

"Mind you, she has reason to hate wars," he went on. "Her father was killed in the Boer War, her brother in the Great War—what a disgusting way to title a war. Great! And now your father's in the Air Force, you say."

"She doesn't even like him," I said bitterly.

"Hmm. Possibly not."

"Well, why not? Why does everyone here seem to dislike him so much? He's—he's a wonderful person."

Charles was silent for such a long time, I thought he was doing a Grandma and refusing to hear me. Then he surprised me by saying, "You know, Katharine, I'm inclined to believe you. You seem an intelligent young woman, and not given to hyperbole. Yes. I think if your father came back to Parsons Creek, people would change their opinion of him. He's probably grown up into a fine person."

112

I could feel my voice go limp as I asked him exactly what it was that my father had done that had made him disliked. He wouldn't tell me but suggested I ask Grandma.

"Your father did nothing to harm me, my dear, or anyone else in this town. He was no villain. He brought sadness to your grandmother and some disappointment to her friends, nothing evil. But it's a private thing, I can't discuss it."

There was another question I thought I might as well clear up, so I put it to him. "Why does Grandma live like this and go out cleaning when she's so wealthy? What happened to all her money?"

He stared at me, then laughed. "Ah! Of course! Tell me, Kate, do you care whether your grandmother is wealthy or not?"

I thought about that for a moment and decided that I didn't really care, Grandma was okay as she was, but I'd like her to be a bit more comfortable.

"That's good." He patted my shoulder. "I can tell you honestly, Mrs. Tucker is not a wealthy woman. Never has been. She's always had to struggle just to survive—but survive she has, with style."

There was one more thing.

"Why should his name be on the honor roll?" Charles said sharply. "Her brother died at Gallipoli, her husband died in the influenza epidemic after the war."

I tottered home. Depressed and defeated. The house felt desolate. I dragged the ill-fated present from under the bed and repacked it.

Mr. Eldershaw was happy to take the wireless back.

"Funny though," he mused, "I thought your grandmother would appreciate a wireless. Keep up with the news. She keeps to herself too much, you know. Needs more company. I do wish she'd . . . Oh well, never mind. She knows. Yes, she knows all right."

As he babbled on, Tom emerged from behind a display of home-bottling cans and said, since it was his time to go off for lunch, he'd walk me home.

I asked him to go with me to the railway station. He introduced me to the dreaded McCann, who checked the return half of my ticket and booked a seat for me back to Sydney in exactly two weeks and two days. I felt I should at least stick to my bargain with Grandma Dawson and wait out the full time, although I deeply longed to flee back to Sydney that very day, dragging my failures behind me.

Then Tom and I walked back to Park Street and I fetched the Sao biscuits from my room. The cheese had hardened around the edges, but they were tasty. We ate them sitting in the pretty little bandstand in the park. We talked about the war, and Tom's chances of getting to England to fly bombers. I didn't want to speak of my father flying Spitfires, nor about my grandfather riding horses at Gallipoli. I didn't want to talk about anything much. It was not a festive meal. When Tom suggested we top the Saos off with a milk shake at the White Rose I had to explain that I couldn't go there ever again, and certainly didn't ever want to speak to Roberto. Or his mother. That was why I'd insisted on walking down the other side of the main street to the railway station. So that I wouldn't even pass the door.

Because Tom was sympathetic I finally blurted out all the horrid details of the previous night's disaster. His sympathy was limited, I found.

"Well, isn't that a funny thing, I never knew your granny was deaf, and I've known her all my life. Cleans house for my mum. Hey, I wonder if my grandfather knows?" I couldn't see that it mattered much whether

Mr. Eldershaw the elder knew or not. "She could be my stepgranny you know, if she wanted. He's been popping the question for years. Says she won't say anything either way. Hey! Maybe she hasn't heard. You think that's likely?" It was the least of my worries.

"And Mrs. Bellini thinks her husband might have been killed in Libya, and it's all my fault." I was sniffing by now. I reminded myself of Mummy and Grandma Dawson. So I did a final big sniff, blinked a couple of times, considered what crying did to my lips, and was in charge again.

"Can't see it's anything to do with you. He's the rat who went back there to fight with them. Funny, he used to be a real friendly guy. Called his milk bar the Vesuvio then. There was this great painting along the wall. A volcano from some place. His old lady and Roberto got rid of it when the war started and put the old name up. The White Rose. It used to be a Greek who owned it. Didn't fool anybody. No one goes there if they can help. Trouble is, it's the only milk bar in town."

I was profoundly sad. Vesuvio seemed such a brave name for a little milk bar, and it didn't seem fair for the town to punish both Roberto and his mother because Mr. Bellini had ratted. But my own problems were more than enough for me. I only wished they'd gone back to Italy with him—that would be one guilt I would have been spared! I took home the empty plate and Tom went back to work. I tried to conjure up my father's voice, but he couldn't fight his way through the mist of resentment I was feeling . . . because of the lies I'd been told about the family.

By my mother! Dad never mentioned them at all! It was my mother who'd told me about my wealthy grandmother and heroic grandfather! *Why?*

I knew who might tell me, if I could get him alone.

19

"I never, ever speak ill of the dead, Katharine, so I shall confine myself to telling you that your grandfath was a liar, a drunkard and a thief. Beyond that I w not go."

I waited, and Roger continued not to speak ill of th dead.

"Rachel came of a very good family, wonderful pe ple, but she had a terrible life with him. He drank eve penny he got his hands on while it was cocky's joy f her and the boy." He noticed my look. "Oh reall Kate! Boiled wheat with a dash of treacle for flavo don't you know anything?"

I really didn't know anything, and didn't really wa to know much more, either, but I had asked and Rog in full flight was hard to stop.

"He worked for Charles's father for a while. Qui an asset I believe until they found him taking mone that didn't belong to him. Charles just never talks abo it, but it was a frightful scandal. Then, during the Fir War, he was in trouble for passing himself off as officer—and he wasn't even in the army! Mind you, be fair he did try to enlist, but they turned him down. Found he had a heart condition. Anyway, he left town when your father was about ten, and Rachel had to bring the boy up alone. She was better off without him actually, if the truth be told. She found later he died in the flu epidemic. More tea, dear?"

I was choking already.

"Oh, now I've upset you. Some people thought he was charming, and I suppose he was, but they were the ones who hadn't been tricked by him. Yet. I'm sorry, dear, but he really was a rotter."

I glugged a bit and he carefully poured another cup of tea for himself. "Now I will say your father was not in the same class as your grandfather. I mean, he wasn't like him at all much. Not anything as bad." Roger showing sympathy and fairness was interesting to watch, his natural inclination being toward acerbity and bias. "It's all very well for those of us who've always been—well, comfortably off. But your father was brought up with no material wealth at all. Lots of love and care, of course, but in extreme poverty. Your granny had to scrape to educate him. She was determined to give him the best chance she could. Well, it went very well while he was at school here, Charles coached him with his work, and there were the books, of course." (I could tell Roger would like them all to come back to their former shelves!) "He did awfully well. Brilliant student."

So what went wrong?

"I suspect it was your mother," Roger confided. "He went to university in Sydney and your granny paid his fees and board. I fancy Charles helped there too, but not a word. You see, there's always been an element of guilt concerning your grandfather. He had such charm that the people he'd wronged felt responsible for him,

117

reasoned that somehow he deserved another chance or some sort of recompense. Believe me, he didn' Anyway, I think that's why Charles did so much fo your father. Now, are you sure you want to hear a this? It is water under the bridge, you know."

It wasn't, not for me, I was still trying to make m way across the river. The going was rough.

"The plan was that he would study law and com back and work in Charles's family firm. Charles wa counting on him. All went well at first, he used to com home in vacation time and study like a beaver over i that bandstand in the park, and he and your grandm got along very well, as they always had. Then one yea when he came home he'd changed. He'd met you mother, you see, from a comfortable North Shore fam ily. Suddenly Parsons Creek seemed a very small, poo place to him, and his mother a small, poor part of hi life. Nothing pleased him here, he was far too gran for anything. He wouldn't even go to collect coal wit his mum."

I felt my ears redden.

"They used to cycle about together, and swim an skate."

Skate?

"They were such good friends, then suddenly he wa in love and his mother . . . well, she was an embar rassment. He never brought *your* mother here to mee her, or us, and he told Charles he couldn't possibl come back to work here. I cannot forgive your fathe for letting Charles down like that. First the father, the the son! But your gran still paid his fees until he grad uated, then of course it was marriage and off to En gland. None of us were asked to the wedding. Afrai we'd spill the beans about his background, I suppose

Goodness knows what fibs your average young man will invent to impress a fiancée, but you can depend on it, being his father's son, he'd have made up a most impressive lineage for himself."

"Oh, that's probably why he went to England, so that he wouldn't have to make up stories anymore . . . he couldn't back down on the stories he'd told Mummy, I suppose. She'd have died." The Dawson grandparents would have been pretty surprised, too.

"First time I've heard of the truth killing anyone."

"You don't know my mother!"

"God is good!" Roger intoned.

I sat on the kitchen floor with my face in the tablecloth and Grandma patted my hair.

"It's all true, of course," she said, "but colored by Roger's character. Reluctant to make allowances for others, is Roger. Your father got carried away by all the grandness. He was clever and witty and good-looking, everything a young man would like to be. But he had no money when he felt he needed it most. It was important to his father and it was important to him, and of course there was nothing I could do to help him there. Except to let him go."

To let him go! She was talking about Grandfather too! Both of them had left her, for the same reason! I sobbed louder and Grandma lifted my head up by the back hair and protested.

"Hey, you're getting my skirt all wet. You have to face the fact, young Kate, people do what they have to do, because of what they are. I had to send him off to university because I wanted my son to have the best education I could afford. Maybe I pushed too hard.

Your father had to make up stories about his life be‐
cause what he had just wasn't enough for him."

"He doesn't now, Grandma. Truly he doesn't. He'
never told me any of this. It was Mummy who told me
about the Light Horse, and you . . ."

"Ah yes, the wealthy widow Tucker," she grinned
"Well, he must have convinced her, then."

He had, perhaps because he'd recognized the need
in Mummy to have a life that was orderly and secure
and sheltered. I couldn't see her in Parsons Creek, col‐
lecting coal.—And skating?

"Oh, skating! I'd almost forgotten the skating. Come
on, let's have a look under here." She hauled me to
my feet and pitched items willy-nilly out of the cupboard
under the sideboard until she was able to drag out two
pairs of heavy metal roller skates.

"It's just like riding a bike," she said. "You never
forget. Tomorrow's Saturday, we'll make a day of it
Forget the housework, we'll skate instead."

So after breakfast next day we set off. I'd long since
given up asking questions of Grandma. She knew what
she was doing, I just followed along. We climbed on
the old bicycle with the skates in the bag up front. I
rode and she clung on behind giving me directions. But
I was surprised when we arrived at our destination. It
was the big grain shed beside the railway line that I'd
noticed as I arrived at Parsons Creek, ten years ago it
seemed.

"Grandma, we mustn't. They'll catch us!"

"Catch us! You scared of that stationmaster? Well
phooey to him, see. This place doesn't even belong to
the railways. It's the farmers' cooperative owns this,
and they're happy for it to be used when they don't
need it. Here, put these on." And she handed me what

I guessed were my father's old roller skates. I strapped and buckled them on over my shoes and she did the same with hers, and off we went.

Grandmother was a very accomplished skater. I was not. Each time I set off, the wheels would shoot out from under me and I'd thump, breathless, onto the hard cement. Laughing, Grandma would haul me up, push me upright, tow me along, until I learned to relax, lean forward into the breeze and let the tiny wheels take me along in great swooping strokes.

We stopped for honey sandwiches and apples and ate them sitting on the grass with our backs resting against the warm wall of the vast wheat silo.

"Used to be a horse stabled in there," Grandma told me. "A big gray draft horse. They used him to pull the railway trucks back and forth when this was a busy junction. He was a dear old horse. Used to crop on the grass here, and your grandpa and I would come down on summer evenings and keep him company. Sometimes I'd gently sit on his back as he walked about. Ah love, they were happy days."

"What was his name, Grandma?" I could see the dear old gray plodding along by the railway track, with a young and beautiful Grandma on his back and her tall handsome love walking along beside her.

Grandma broke my dream with her husky laugh. "We called him Rosinante, which was quite an appropriate name, as things turned out. Come on, race you to the other end!"

And we were off again, careering up and down the concrete area, clicking over the cracks and crashing into the wall at the other end. Then we held hands and together we whizzed and zoomed, laughed and shouted, through the lengthening shadows of the echoing shed.

Grandma suggested I pedal the bike home too. That way I could stand up and pedal and give my aching bottom a rest. I didn't tell her that my knees were twanging with a monumental pain as well. But it had been such a splendid day that I sang all the way back.

I knew exactly what I wanted to do next, so after I'd bathed I brought out my compendium and began a letter to my father.

Grandma was shelling peas for dinner. "Might upset them, you know. Suddenly finding out you're here. With me."

"I want to, Grandma. Right now."

"Ho, Miss Impetuous. You know, your grandfather was a wonderful man."

That wasn't the story I'd heard.

"Had his faults, mind. Gambled, drank, couldn't be relied on, but ah, Katharine, he was fun to be with! If only you could find such a husband. A little steadier, of course!"

I thought "a little steadier" might be more comfortable too, but Grandpa was beginning to sound more lovable than Roger had described him to be.

"He wanted to do so much for David and me, but he always set his sights too high." Grandma's voice went quiet. "He could never believe that I loved him just as he was." Her voice rose again and her eyes focused on me once more. "Anyway, as I was saying, Miss Impetuous, he was a wonderful man and he helped me a lot. I was a willful young thing and he used to say, 'Now, Rachel, be still! And think!' Saved me from many a blunder, I can tell you."

Me too.

I was still and I thought it most appropriate that I should write to my father on that day, when I'd really met his mother for the first time. And his father.

I decided to send the letter direct to his air force address, then he could show it to Mummy when he saw her if he wanted to. I told him all the happy things, but couldn't yet mention collecting coal, surprise parties, the War Memorial, his mother's deafness. But I knew I'd be able to soon. When I'd almost come to a stop, Grandma prodded me with the blunt end of her potato knife. "You could say his mother sends her love."

"You said you didn't like him!"

"What's that got to do with the price of eggs? Liking and loving are two vastly different things. Don't you know that?"

"Well, why don't you say it yourself?" I passed the pen and the compendium across to her. She glared at me for a while, then poked her tongue out from between her teeth and began to write, very slowly at first, choosing her words with care, then on and on for a full page.

That night in my room I took the letter out of its envelope to read what Grandma had written about me. I reread my letter first and when I came to her part a strange thing happened and I just didn't want to read any further. It was a feeling I'd never had before. Reading other people's letters is perfectly all right with me. How else can you know what they really think about you? Like listening at doors. If the chance occurs you snatch it. But just this one time I didn't want to, though that's not to say I won't do it again whenever I choose.

So I folded it all up and stuck down the envelope. I wanted to tell Grandma I hadn't read it, but by morning it didn't seem really important. So I didn't mention it, just trotted up to the post office, slipped it into the slot, and whispered "Sealed with a loving kiss" as it disappeared from view.

20

If I had been granted three wishes, two of them would have been that I needn't ever see Roberto Bellini again. Ever. My toes curled and my ears burned with mortification each time I remembered the look he'd given me as he and his mother left after the Great Surprise Party.

So I decided to get it over with straightaway.

I also had to spend the five pounds on a present for Grandma.

So one day, after she had set off for work, I started on my mission. The Emporium first, where Mr. Eldershaw bobbed and smiled and Tom emanated like a genie from behind a display of slow combustion stoves. Eldershaw the Elder then disappeared into Ladies' Shoes and Tom and I were alone. He suggested a picnic, just the two of us, and I thought about it. It could be a handy point-scoring topic of conversation with Cathy and the other girls back at school in Sydney.

"Just the two of us?" I checked. But when he said yes with an anticipatory grin I said I really didn't think I'd have time.

"Half a day. Your gran won't mind. Tell her it's where we rigged the rope on the tree to swing out into the river."

"You want me to swing . . . out . . . ?"

"Nah. We do that in summertime. It's pretty safe. Your gran chose the spot. It's where they swam when your dad was a kid."

I believed him, but pleaded it was too cold for picnics and I really had a lot to do. He took the refusal very pleasantly and agreed to help me choose Grandma's gift. Suddenly he turned from the old customer evader into a regular salesman, bringing all sorts of suggestions over to the counter for my consideration. I sat on the high-backed chair and considered them as I had seen my mother do. There was an electric toaster for nineteen shillings and eleven pence, an electric jug for the same price, a marvelous gadget that Tom was particularly proud of, called the Meteor Glass Blow-fly Trap for 15/6, and a beautiful tea set for 37/6. But then, on the shelf behind him, I saw the perfect present.

It was called the Aurolese. *(Specially designed to alleviate the strain of nerve deafness—tinnitus. With its use a magnification of the actual voice itself is heard, not merely a reproduction, and no wires or batteries are required. The ability to function perfectly does not depreciate with age. Priced from seven guineas to eleven guineas, according to power.)*

The insurance money that Grandpa Dawson had given me was almost untouched. A couple of malted milks and a few chocolate bars had been my only purchases, so I was well able to afford the cheaper model. Tom nipped around the back of the counter and pulled down the little cage from its overhead wires, popped the money and docket in it and pulled the cord that sent it pinging across the shop to the cashier's roost above the hardware department. Then he wrapped the box with tense precision. No wonder he didn't look for customers; I was beginning to understand that customers wouldn't seek him out either. The time it took him to assess the length of brown paper that had to be torn off by the serrated metal cutter that hinged above the roll! Then the corners of the parcel had to match exactly. The string was pulled and looped, stretched and twisted, my finger was borrowed to hold the first knot in place, and then a double loop was devised so that I could hitch a finger in it to carry the parcel home. By the time he'd finished his laborious task the little cage was shivering angrily at the end of its wire and he took it down, unscrewed the lid and triumphantly handed me my change and receipt.

It seemed ages since I'd come into the shop and I considered going straight home without calling at the White Rose. But the Aurolese would give me an excuse to be there. I didn't want Roberto to be thinking I'd made a special trip. So I turned away from Park Street and, feeling sick, crept toward the milk bar.

He was there, of course, he was always there, and as always he was glaring morosely through the doorway as I entered.

I took a deep breath and made a firm decision to keep the conversation strictly on Grandma's Aurolese until he decided to talk about something else, such as the party, or one of our fathers, or what a thoughtless idiot I'd been, upsetting his mother with the war broadcast. I would definitely leave the choice of topic to him.

So I marched up to the counter, put the parcel down beside the till and began my calm conversation.

"How was I to know . . . I can't be expected . . . It's

not my fault your father went over there . . . My father . . . I didn't know . . . truly . . . I'm not . . ."

He slowly moved his gaze from the footpath back inside to me, and while his expression didn't change, at least he spoke. Stopping me in midwail.

"What's the matter with you?" I might have been a complete stranger he'd never seen before in his life. "You want a malted?"

I nodded, groping for my hanky.

"Well then, if you want a malted you have a malted, but we don't need hysterics. Okay? Caramel, isn't it?"

At least he remembered *that*, so I decided to try again.

"Look," I began, "I've come to apologize. So I apologize. Will you tell your mother I didn't mean to upset her?"

"Okay. You didn't mean to upset her. I'll tell her. You apologized to your granny yet? That was a pretty lousy trick you played on her you know. Not classy enough for you, eh? So you go and do a rotten thing like that. You're certainly not . . ."

"I know," I said, "I'm not the man my granny is."

"Too right you're not," he agreed, a mite too fast for my liking. "When someone's deaf you don't pull a stunt like that on them. How'd you like it if . . ."

"I didn't know, and will you stop, please? You don't have to go on. I feel rotten enough about it already."

He flung the glass and the metal container down on the counter and I flung a straw in and began to suck. Then I started again.

"Look, Roberto, I'm sorry for the trouble I caused. Gran knows now that I didn't mean . . . well, anyway, I'm sorry about your father being in Libya and all that."

He made himself a milk shake then. Just a plain old

127

vanilla milkshake, which I thought was a great shame, with all those delicious flavors going free, to say nothing of the malt.

"We don't know where he is," he told me, after he'd taken his first sip. "My mother just goes to pieces like that whenever she hears anything at all about the war. I want to enlist when I'm eighteen, but how can I? She'd drop down dead at my feet if I even mentioned it. She's very excitable."

That was true. And noisy with it!

"It must be awfully difficult for you."

The glare came back. "She's okay. We're all right. When the war's over I'm going back to Italy anyway . . . sell up this place . . . not going to stick around in this dump . . . soon as I can, I'm off."

"But you were born here, weren't you? You said you wanted to enlist. Just now. You said that."

He took his drink farther up on his side of the counter, muttering over his shoulder as he went, "None of your business, is it?"

I poured the rest of my malted into my glass, collected my handbag and Grandma's Aurolese, and followed him.

"You're right. It is none of my business. But would you please listen to me for another minute, because there's something that's none of your business either, but I would like to tell you, if you don't mind."

He waited. I guessed he was listening.

"It's about my father. He's not a fighter pilot at all. I really don't know why I said he was. He is in the air force, but he's only ground staff. No medals, no Germans shot down and quite definitely no Italians. He's just an ordinary man, with glasses and not much hair. But he's a very . . . he's a remarkably good father."

128

"I knew," he replied coldly. "I knew all the time he was no big hero. You lay it on too thick. Well, let me tell you something. My old man's a remarkably good father too, you'd better believe it. And so's my mother."

I decided not to ask his advice about the Aurolese, he didn't seem to be in the right mood just then, so I gathered up my things, paid for my malted, and trudged off home. The visit had not been the success I had planned. But I was proving to be an outstandingly clumsy planner anyway.

As I walked along Park Street I decided that I might as well round things off, so I went to the door of the Bellinis' house and knocked. The curtain at the window twitched and Mrs. Bellini opened the door. She wasn't too happy to see me either; she looked as if she expected me to announce the defeat of the entire Italian army or something just as shattering. But she bravely invited me in. The inside of the house was marvelously colorful, with pictures of cherubs and hearts on the walls and a statue of a lady saint on the sideboard, with a big vase of paper flowers on each side of it. The smell of whatever she put in that lasagne stuff was right through the house. Delectable! I thought it wise not to mention the party too soon in my visit, in case Mrs. Bellini, reminded of the war, fractured into pieces again, so I showed her the parcel and asked her what she thought of it as a gift for Grandma. She obviously did not think much of it. She spelled out the words on the box, asked me what is *tinnitus*, and when I explained that it was another way of saying deafness, she wanted to know if *tinnitus* was the sort of deafness that my nonna had. Deaf was deaf as far as I knew, so I said yes, it was, and we repacked the box.

I was longing for tea but she made coffee, very thick

and strong. My first cup actually, and I didn't like it. But she served yummy little almond biscuits, and nodded and smiled to encourage me to eat more.

"I make for Roberto," she said, "but he not eat much. He work too hard, but what can we do? Is good boy. Is lovely boy."

I nodded, agreeing that he worked hard, not with the bit about him being a lovely boy, and I had to smile, thinking of the expression there would be on his face if he heard his mother describe him so.

Mrs. Bellini talked on and on. I guess shutting herself up in the house all day gave her plenty of time to think of things she wanted to talk about when she finally did let loose. I was happy to listen and nod, although her accent was so strong at times that I no doubt nodded agreement when I should have been shaking in vehement denial. After all, she was an Italian, with a husband on the other side.

The Bellini family, I was interested to hear, had shared in most of Grandma's pastimes before the war. She had shown them where to roller-skate, had taught Roberto to swim (and swing into the river on a rope, I presume). And, of course, she had advised them on the best places to collect coal. That woman was certainly a strong force in Parsons Creek.

Finally I collected my things and went home, with Mrs. Bellini's voice continuing to make my ears twang for some time. I might have begun to feel sorry for Roberto if I hadn't disliked him so much.

21

Katharine Tucker crashes to ground again! I can understand why some people give up trying to please other people. I wish I could myself.

I gave the present to Grandma after dinner. No flourishes this time, no party, no audience. Slowly she unwrapped it, carefully rewinding the string around two fingers, tying it in a little bow and hanging it on the hook behind the cupboard door before she spread out the wrapping paper. Tom would have been pleased with the respect she was paying his parcel!

She stared at the box for a few minutes, whispering "Aurolese" over and over as if to get the pronunciation right, then she started to rock back and forth in her chair. Hooting with laughter! At times she would catch her breath and whisper "Aurolese . . . *tinnitus* . . ." and wipe her eyes, then go off again with another peal.

When she began to slow down I said, "I've done it again, haven't I?" in a cool and distant tone. There is a limit to what I am prepared to accept in the way of ridicule and with Grandma and Roberto Bellini, I felt this day's quota had been achieved already.

She calmed down, and hiccupping now and then, explained that she'd been to doctors about her hearing, there was absolutely nothing they could do to help her, and the device I was offering would just be something she'd have to remember to carry about with her and not to lose, and it certainly wouldn't help her to hear any better. Specially since *tinnitus* wasn't what she had.

"Anyway," she asked defensively, "what's the matter with lip-reading? I hear everything I want to with that, thanks all the same. A sight more than I want to sometimes, come to that." Then she leaned across the table and took my face in her hands. "You're a kind child, Katharine. You've a good heart in that flat little chest of yours. This money your gran gave you has become a bit of a nuisance, hasn't it? A heavy responsibility."

My chest *is* flat. Flattish. But I'm doing exercises for that.

"I'm giving up now," I said. "Mr. Eldershaw's Emporium will be full of secondhand goods if I keep on buying things and taking them back."

"I'll take it back for you," she offered. "Paul Eldershaw and I will have a good laugh. You and his Tom are a great pair of shoppers."

"Mr. Eldershaw doesn't know you can't hear," I reminded her, but she didn't seem to think it mattered, just shrugged. "Thought he did. Oh well, he'll know now, won't he?"

And she retrieved the string and paper and repacked the parcel. I took the stupid hearing aid back to Mr. Eldershaw myself and the realization that Grandma was deaf cleared the jovial smile right off his face. I could see him thinking of all the times he'd proposed to her and had no answer . . . because she didn't even know the question was being popped.

I waited, and sure enough, he came around to thinking that because she hadn't heard the question, she hadn't in fact ever refused. I smiled with him as hope and his own smile returned to him.

"You have to stand where she can look at your lips move, Mr. Eldershaw. Then she knows everything you say."

"I will, I will," he breathed, as if he was already at the altar with Grandma by his side. He nipped across to the cashier's pen to collect my refund himself, not trusting the flying contraption any more than he trusted his staff to make sales without his help.

So there I was with the money back in my purse and still no present bought for Grandma. So after dinner that night I asked her what she'd like me to spend it on. I had lost my nerve completely.

When she told me what she wanted I didn't like the idea at all and said so, but she turned her head away to pretend she hadn't heard.

"It's going to be very difficult to do that, Grandma," I pleaded. "Impossible, actually. And I'm only here for another week and a day."

"Well, it'll have to be this Saturday then, won't it? I hadn't realized you'd be off so soon."

I didn't mean to end up in a heap again, but I did. Being still and thinking only worked for me on some occasions.

"Come on, now." Grandma smiled. "Think I didn't know? I knew you weren't planning to stay forever. You were prudent to book your seat early. You've got to get back to school. Education's very important, Katharine. You get yourself a good education and you can do anything in the world you want."

I told her what I wanted was to stay in Parsons Creek,

133

and my ears were quite surprised to hear it. But she was determined.

"No. Sydney's where your mother wanted you to be, and that's where I want you to be, young lady. Doesn't matter where you are, so long as I've got you in here." And she patted her navy woolly jumper. "Now, come along, we have some planning to do."

So I fetched my compendium and fountain pen and we made lists. One for her, one for me and one general one to be left on the shelf in the kitchen to remind us of what had still to be done.

The next day I doubled Grandma to work on the bicycle then continued on alone. As I left her at the gate of the house she was cleaning that day she groped in her pocket, took out the piece of paper that contained her list, read it carefully, popped it back into the pocket, tipped me a salute, and marched up the path.

I pedaled out of town and along the road I remembered to Norths' farm. The yard was just as noisy as usual, animals everywhere and abandoned parts of old farm machinery jutting up through the dirt.

Mrs. North almost carried me inside to the kitchen, and although I swore I was in a hurry and couldn't stay, we managed a few cups of tea and she happened to be putting some scones in the oven that she wanted my opinion of, so it was the middle of the day before I arrived home again. I stabled the bicycle and walked down to Eldershaw's Emporium. Both the male Eldershaws bobbed up to greet me as if I were an old and valued customer rather than a nuisance who had bought only two articles so far, and returned both!

I spoke to Eldershaw Senior first. The expression of expectancy and joy on his little round red face was wondrous to see. It glowed even stronger when I offered him another chance to speak to his beloved, this time away from the confines of the shop.

"Delighted," beamed the little face, "delighted, delighted."

I had to interrupt his delight to hand him a list, with the prices set down beside each item. He took a big red pencil from his pocket, and with a flourish drew a line down the column of numbers!

"My pleasure. A pleasure, a pleasure." I hoped he wasn't going to talk forever in triplicate from here on. Grandma might grow impatient at having to read each message three times. His generosity also left me with my present-money still to be spent. I didn't know how to *insist* on paying for the stuff.

Tom refused to be involved at all and was quite sulky about it. "I won't be in it, thanks. Anyway, I'm off in a few weeks, to enlist. Do my bit, you know."

"Been reading too many of those recruiting posters," his grandfather complained. "They won't take him, you know, they'll find out about his feet."

I looked at Tom's feet. They seemed quite ordinary to me.

"Flat!" their grandfather exulted. "Runs in the family. Me, his father, his uncle, we've all got flat feet. Doesn't stand a chance!"

"My father wears glasses, he can't see a thing without them, and they took him in the Royal Air Force. Ground crew." I listened to myself with astonishment. Boasting about how ordinary my father was!

Mr. Eldershaw was miffed but Tom acknowledged the support I'd given him by escorting me to the timber-yard out the back where we selected a smooth plank of eight by two, about five feet long. Then I chose the paints—Grandma had brushes at home—and Tom car-

135

ried the whole lot back to the house for me and stowed it in the shed.

My job was an exacting one and took up just about all my time for the rest of the week. Roger popped in every now and again to check on my work and advise. Industry had certainly missed out on an expert foreman when Roger took up music as a career!

When she arrived home at night, Grandma would report her successes, or failures, mostly successes, and on Friday night she was up until midnight with the kitchen trembling with heat from the stove, and the table piled high with cooling apple tartlets and blackberry pies.

I was elsewhere. In next door with Mrs. Bellini, fighting one of the hardest battles of my life. Actually the main problem was getting her to be quiet long enough to allow me to say my piece. When I did she leaped straight into a conniption. With my own mother I shouldn't have been surprised, would have known how to cope. Finally I took Mrs. Bellini by the shoulders and shook her, just a little bit.

"Mrs. Bellini," I shouted, "be still!" Startled, she was still, and blessedly silent. "Now think!" Whether she actually thought or not I don't know, but her silence was as much as I could hope for.

"Roberto has too much work to do. You said so yourself." She nodded. "If you love Roberto you will do it." She nodded. "It's Grandma's idea, she wants it." She nodded again. "The people in this town are good, decent people, really." She didn't quite manage the nod this time, but she remained silent. "This war's not going to last forever," I pleaded, praying the word wouldn't start her up again before I'd managed to convince her. "Bellini is a famous, great Italian name," I

136

enthused and she leaned on my shoulder and sobbed. I was running out of arguments. "Mrs. Bellini, please!" She sobbed louder. I gave up, Grandma would have to do it. As I opened the door I turned and bellowed in anger, "All right, Mrs. Bellini, what if your husband doesn't come back? What's going to happen to you and Roberto? Think about that!"

I marched out and helped Grandma roll pastry for the rest of the evening, not knowing if I'd been successful or not.

"You worry too much, Katharine," Gran said as she slapped another tray of tarts onto the table. "Things usually work out reasonably well, for someone anyway, no matter how much fretting we do."

I checked our lists again and yelped, "We'll need a ladder! Grandma, we haven't a ladder!" I ran around the table and said it again where she could hear me.

"Eldershaw's bringing a ladder."

"What time did you tell your list?"

"Settle, will you? I told them six o'clock. That's two hours before the pictures start at the School of Arts. Now, you figure there's enough tarts? And stop sampling them, will you? There'll be none left for the others."

So we went weary to bed and next morning she was up with the fire ablaze by six and with a tray of savory pastries already browning in the oven.

By eleven I was a trembling wreck. I knocked on Mrs. Bellini's door, ready to fling my arms around her knees and beg if necessary. She opened the door and glared at me.

"I busy. I too busy to talk." I tottered backward with wonder. "I make lasagne. You tell your nonna. I make lasagne."

I staggered home to study the lists again. Grandma refused to look at me at all. In some ways deaf people could be said to have an advantage. No matter how loudly you screech they can close you off completely whenever they want to and get on with what they're doing without interruption, just by closing their eyes. I came close to punching my grandmother a few times that day!

Roger came in about two, rubbing his hands. I think we both regretted our conversation about my family, and I sensed his eagerness to make amends.

"Isn't this fun?" he chortled. "Even Charles approves . . . I say, Rachel, you've completely outclassed me. All I've done is some wretched little iced cakes!"

He was lying. I knew that between trips to the bicycle shed to chivvy me he'd been madly busy baking and decorating with a piping nozzle and an icing bag. All week long.

He knew that I knew, and he grinned at me over Grandma's shoulder, and suddenly I liked him a lot.

"I don't suppose anyone'll notice if they're terribly bad, Roger," I murmured, and grinned back at him.

As Grandma said, people do what they have to do, because of being what they are. I must remember to think about that very seriously sometime.

22

By five o'clock we were ready. I'd put on my best skirt and sweater and Gran had changed into her brightest tablecloth and her largest blue jumper. Her tennis shoes had been whitened and she had a fresh red ribbon in her hair. She looked beautiful.

At a quarter to six there was a knock on the door and a sheepish Tom Eldershaw trudged down the hall.

"Come to give a hand," he muttered. "Not staying, mind, just came to help you with the stuff."

I was grateful, knowing what an effort it must be for him. I took him to the shed and collected our burden, then the three of us started out, Grandma leading with a baker's basket full of assorted pastries with a large check tea towel over them. At the Bellinis' gate Tom and I waited while Grandma banged on the door and shouted, "Bella! Bella! *Avanti!*" and Bella finally avantied, sobbing, "No! Rachel! *Ah dio!* No, I cannot do it!"

I don't know what Grandma said to her, but at last she did join us, bearing her burden, the oven tray with its aromatic contents, and a basket of almond biscuits.

Around the corner into the main street we trooped, past the bank, the general store, the butcher, the fruit shop, all closed, and then we were at the entrance to the White Rose milk bar.

Mrs. Bellini ran inside, tearfully assuring a startled Roberto that she hadn't wanted to come, it hadn't been her idea, and she was going back home now. *Subito!*

I would have willingly joined her. My plummeting stomach and sweaty palms told me I'd done it again. Parsons Creek would be a more tranquil place when I returned to Sydney.

But I had no chance of retreating. A large motorcar swept along the street, stopped and backed to park at the curb outside the milk bar. Out stepped Mr. Eldershaw and his son and daughter-in-law, Tom's parents. They untied a stepladder from the running board and set it up beneath the White Rose and Tom went up and began to unhook the shop sign. Poor Roberto, he longed to protest and was afraid to. If his mother hadn't been there I think he would have dragged Tom down the ladder and punched him. Or maybe it was a combination of circumstances that forced him to stand and watch without a struggle. The fact that his father was fighting on the other side, and that the townspeople resented the presence of him and his mother. Possibly also the fact that Grandma was standing directly in front of him holding an enormous baker's basket full of pies as if she was prepared to flatten him with the basket and bury him beneath a hill of pies if he moved!

No one said a word and finally the new sign was up. VESUVIO, it said in bright red letters, and in smaller blue ones, *Café*, Milk Bar. Roger had suggested lots of gold curlicues and I had to admit they did add the right touch. I was pleased with it.

"Take it down," Roberto hissed. "Why? Why did you do that? Take it down!"

140

"Take it down yourself if you want to!" Tom stowed the ladder and the old sign by his father's car and stood belligerently in the doorway. They glared at each other and Mrs. Bellini bawled: "Such good friends they were at school!"

I couldn't see that her remark would help much, and it didn't. They each turned to glare at her.

"Well, I'm off then." Tom strode away down the street. His parents and grandfather shuffled about, no doubt feeling extremely embarrassed, as I did, but just then a hubbub approached, a jubilation of voices.

Like a victorious football team they tumbled in through the doorway.

Roger was in the lead, then Charles, and they had brought along a nicely selected group of townspeople. I recognized some of them from my mooching about town. Miss Carter from the telephone exchange, the bank manager, the sergeant of police and the matron of the local hospital. The rest were strangers to me. Roger advanced to the counter and set down his trays of splendidly decorated cakes, and simply because there were so many people milling about, Roberto was obliged to look more pleasant and step back behind the counter.

Then a sulky drew up beside the Eldershaws' car and Mrs. North clambered down, patted the horse's rump and came inside followed by her enormous husband and the "boys," each of them elderly and bearded and roughly the same size as a piano. Each a tribute to Mrs. North's cooking skills. They carried in the food Mrs. North had promised me, and the party got under way.

I followed Grandma and Mrs. Bellini out the back and there was a huge oven, big enough to heat up all the food. We set out plates of pies and cakes and topped up the vast urn for tea and coffee later. Preparations were completed in a short time, but Mrs. Bellini and I were of the same mind, we both kept our heads well down and fussed about polishing glasses with tea towels and counting knives and forks over and over again. I could see that Grandma was growing impatient with our delays, but I wanted desperately to be somewhere else!

She turned to check the oven, so I slid across to the door at the back and quietly opened it. It did not lead to an exit as I had hoped, but to a narrow storeroom. Shelves along one side held tins of malt and sugar, coffee and tea, and bottles of flavoring. Along the opposite wall a set of canvasses was propped. I turned them over and saw that each formed a section of a long painting. It was a picture of a peaceful countryside, green fields, olive groves, red geraniums, farmhouses with tiled roofs and faded sienna walls. And in the background, the focus of it all, the towering volcano. Vesuvio! So Roberto had kept it all this time, hidden away, but not destroyed.

Grandma called, "Katharine, if you're not out of there and inside that milk bar in three seconds I'll tan your hide for you. This is your party, remember."

"It is not! It was all your idea!" I remembered just in time to dash out and face her as I spoke.

"My idea? What nonsense. Everyone knows I can't tolerate parties. Why would I suggest such a thing. Come along now, I want you to meet my friends." And she took my hand and grasped Mrs. Bellini firmly by her arm and marched us back to the rest of the guests.

Grandma worked for some of them, and one of the jobs on her list had been to persuade them to come along. I guessed that not many of them would have argued with her. Grandma could be very persuasive when she wanted something, and they seemed very fond

142

of her. My mother had chars who did the housework back in England, but none of them stayed very long, Mummy always suspected that they stole things. I don't think they did, we were all pretty careless of our things, but none of them became friends, as Grandma seemed to be with her ladies.

Roger was enjoying himself hugely, jollying people along and moving them around like a choreographer with the ballet.

"Come over here by the door, Mrs. North. I want the people going to the cinema to see how popular the place is. Charles, you must sit by Matron, tell her about your operation! Roberto, could we please have some more lemon squashes over here."

He actually did entice lots more people in. Some going home from the hotels and others on their way up town to the School of Arts for the evening show. They stared, wondering what was going on, then diffidently stepped over the threshold and were snatched by the delighted Roger, who led them to the counter, pressed cakes and pies on them and supervised while they bought chocolates and sweets to take with them, all the time assuring them that the Vesuvio would be the most popular and hospitable meeting place in town from this day onward.

The combination of free food and Roger's enthusiasm persuaded many of them to stay and join the party. But some only came in out of curiosity, and when they saw that Roberto was still in charge and the café had not changed hands, they left. A few of them were quite rude, but Charles shushed me when I tried to reason with them.

"This is a party, remember?" he whispered. "They don't have to stay if they don't want to."

So they went. But trade was brisk, the till was pinging

happily and Mrs. Bellini and Roberto were working like crazy pouring drinks and giving change. After slinking about in the background for a while I decided that since I was there anyway and Grandma wouldn't let me go home, I might as well do something, so I carried glasses and plates from counter to table, washed up in the kitchen out back and restocked the shelves and refrigerator. After a while I felt quite comfortable and even spoke to a few people, if they spoke to me first. An evening such as this, where things seemed to be going smoothly, was outside my previous experience!

Grandma presided at a table toward the back and I noticed how thoughtfully each person came to her, sat in the booth opposite, and chatted to her. Only Charles would have had the sensitivity and forethought to tell all of those who didn't already know, that Grandma needed to see words before she could hear them. Old Mr. Eldershaw spent a lot of time near her, hovering.

At about eight o'clock Roger took one of the metal milk shake containers and a spoon and clanged us all into silence.

"Your attention please, ladies and gentlemen," he trumpeted. "Charles has a little speech to deliver. Pray silence for Mr. . . . Charles . . . Hope!"

Mrs. Bellini, transformed into a beaming hostess, dashed forward with an empty soft-drink box for Charles to stand on, and he began:

"Friends, thank you all for coming. Tonight we celebrate a very happy moment in the history of Parsons Creek. Because our dear Rachel Tucker and her beautiful granddaughter, Katharine, had a kind and generous thought, we, who normally lead private and somewhat selfish lives, have been persuaded to come here and show our friendship and support, not just for

144

the Bellinis, but for each other. We all remember Aldo Bellini, he brought much warmth and genuine love to this town. It was a sadness for him, and for us his friends, when he had to return to Italy to see his dying mother. He arrived there as war broke out and was, we fear, conscripted into one of the Italian armed forces."

I longed with all the yearning that my soul possessed for a small cataclysm, one that would create a fissure in the floor beneath my feet, that I could silently fall through, never to be seen again. Roberto's father *hadn't* gone to volunteer to fight with the enemy. He'd just happened to go at the wrongest time of all.

Charles was still talking. "Roberto is an Australian, born here, and Rosa is our dear friend. In Aldo's absence we, the people of Parsons Creek, are responsible for Aldo's family, just as we feel responsible for all the families of all those who are fighting in this hellish war. We pride ourselves on this feeling of responsibility, yet I feel that we have failed the Bellinis. Because of apathy, we have failed to show that we care about them. Tonight will change that. We want you all to persuade your friends, as you have been persuaded, to come to the Vesuvio and help Rosa and Roberto to feel comfortable again in this community. No longer need they hide behind the poignant pretense that they are the Bells and that this milk bar is the White Rose. They are the Bellinis! It is the Vesuvio!"

After that everyone milled around the Bellinis and Grandma and me and I started to feel better. I came back to the counter with empty glasses and Roberto was smiling. Not at me exactly, but it was good to see his face without its customary scowl. I waited until he looked at me.

"Roberto," I said, "are you still angry about the sign?

Because I can ask Tom to take it down tomorrow, if you like."

"I'll think about it," he answered. "See how things go. It's been a good night, but I don't expect any miracles. These people will tell their friends, and maybe, just maybe, the town might change its attitude, but I don't hold out much hope."

"They want to be friendly, truly they do."

"Sure. They called my parents 'reffos' when they first came to Australia, then 'dagoes.' Some of them called us 'the Greeks,' because to them anyone who runs a milk bar must be Greek! But things are improving. You're right, they do want to be friendly. Now they call us 'Eyeties,' so at least they acknowledge that we're Italian."

"You're not Italian, Roberto. You're Australian."

"Sorry. I keep forgetting." His scowl was back again. I seemed to have a very flattening effect on Roberto. He shrugged. "Well, anyway, it's been a great party." I waited. He looked at me for a moment, then muttered "Thanks," and walked away.

Suddenly I was absolutely desolate. I was leaving in three days and suddenly Parsons Creek seemed to be such an interesting place to be. I'd wasted three weeks and four days.

Roberto stacked his tray of goodies ready for the cinema intermission. After he'd gone we all cleaned the place up and the guests drifted off home. Mr. Eldershaw stayed behind while Grandma and I washed up, then he walked Grandma and me home. When we arrived I pleaded complete exhaustion and went to bed. They sat in the kitchen and talked for hours.

146

23

The next day was Sunday. I didn't expect Roberto to drop in and say how great the party had been, so I wasn't a bit disappointed when he didn't. But it was a busy day. Tom came around during the morning and we sat on the back step in the sun to talk.

"Wish I wasn't going off to enlist now," he complained. "Met this marvelous girl last night. At a party." He flicked an eye at me to see what my reaction would be. I wondered if I should sob, gnaw my lip to demonstrate the depths of my unrequited love, or fling myself on his manly chest and pant out words of yearning. He had been decent about putting up the sign for me. I compromised.

"Congratulations," I said. "Just as well you didn't stay at our party, then. It was a great success, but no girls there, I'm afraid."

"Huh. Great. That's great. That Roberto Bellini needs to smarten himself up a bit though. I could have knocked him down last night. Would have if all those people hadn't been there. He has some nerve, for an alien."

I wondered if there would be time enough to persuade

Tom that there were more similarities between him and Roberto than there were differences. Both born in Parsons Creek, about the same age, both stubborn and difficult to get on with, both very pleasant to be with. I was glad I hadn't said it out loud because the last bit just was not true. Roberto was not at all pleasant to be with. I'd never been in his company for more than four minutes without hating him and having an argument. But I did tell Tom about Roberto's father going to Italy to see his mother just as the war broke out. He didn't believe me.

"Nah. He went to Italy to enlist. That's just a story they put around. There's internment camps for enemy aliens here you know. Roberto and his mum don't want to go to one of those, so that's why they put that story around. Nah, take it from me. He went to enlist."

And apart from admitting grudgingly that Aldo Bellini had been a decent sort of bloke, he wouldn't budge from his opinion. So I gave up. It was the people who were staying on in the town who had to be persuaded to give the Bellinis a chance, not the ones who were leaving. Tom suggested we go for a ride on the bikes, or skating. I said I didn't want to go out. He wondered if it mightn't be pleasant to go across to the park and sit in the rotunda in the sun. I certainly didn't want to do that, the rotunda was in full view of anyone who might be walking along Park Street, or looking out from one of the houses or something like that. So he wandered off, no doubt to visit the mythical girl he'd met at the party.

I went to the back of the shed and had another look at the beehive, wishing it was summer so that I could help Grandma steal the honey. No bees were out, but I could hear them thrumming about inside the hive.

Selfishly busy. I walked around the side of the house and that reminded me of the boys with their paint on my first night at Parsons Creek. So I decided to knock on the Bellinis' door and see how Mrs. Bellini was, and if there was anything I could do to help her.

This time no curtains twitched, no one whispered from behind the closed door. There was no one at home. I was sorry I'd bothered, but as I came out of the Bellinis' gate a woman walking past said:

"Nobody there, dear. Saw them at Mass this morning and they stayed on." Of course, Italians, they'd be Roman Catholics.

"Lovely to see them back. You know they haven't hardly been to church since Aldo left."

I walked along with her awhile, she seemed an interesting and knowledgeable woman.

"Father Ryan spoke about Aldo this morning. You won't believe this, but we even prayed for him! Seems funny, doesn't it? Praying for someone on the other side, who's maybe killing our boys over there. And he seemed such a nice man, Aldo. Believe there was a party on at the White Rose last night, to sort of buck the Bellinis up. Bellini! Funny, you know, anyone new to town they've been telling they're called Bell! Never fooled anyone, mind. They was always the Bellinis to me. Mind you, I always liked Rosa. Might drop in to the café now and again. Now she's back."

I left her then. She made it sound as if Mrs. Bellini had been away for a holiday, rather than hiding inside her own house for fear of being hurt.

I went inside, patting a few gnomes as I passed. Grandma was sitting in a sunny corner of the back veranda stitching tiny pieces of cloth together. She'd only just begun work on it, but it looked as if it might grow into another patchwork quilt like the one on my bed. I hoped she might be making it for me. On the table beside her there was a cardboard box with *Sunlight Soap* stenciled on its side. It was full of brightly colored materials, so I sat on the floor at her feet and cut out shapes with her enormous steel scissors and the tiny metal templates she gave me. Then I set some of them out on the floor to see which colors and patterns went best together. I began to understand what delight Grandma must have experienced painting the bricks of the house, and I told her so.

"Yes," she said, "it saddens me that it could never be so much fun again."

"But you could paint it again, Grandma."

"Ah no, my dear, it wouldn't be the same. It was a marvelous game of surprises then. But next time I'd know what colors I had."

It was a relaxed and shiny time. We were alone together on our tiny island of winter sunshine. So I asked her. At last.

"I keep them as a reminder," she told me. "They rightfully belong to your father. Oh yes, they're David's gnomes. Not that he's likely to come and claim them, but you never know! In the meantime, they don't give much trouble."

I waited, still sorting colors and shapes.

"It was when your father was at university, just before he met your mother. A sign, I suppose, that he wasn't really happy here, that he needed more than Parsons Creek could offer. He suddenly wanted to make a lot of money, you see, and the stupid bank manager convinced him he could make a fortune selling garden decorations. There *was* a big interest in gardens then, but I never could believe people'd pay good money for statues to stand around and do nothing. Still, I went

150

along with the plan. He was a pretty convincing arguer I can tell you, same as his father used to be. So we spent a deal of money we could ill afford on buying a mold and bags of cement and paints, and we spent all his long vacation out in that shed at the back, manufacturing flipping garden gnomes."

"And?"

"Cut me some more of that blue, please, dear. Well, the problem was, when he came home for his next holiday—and that was the last time he did come home—nobody wanted to buy, and he wasn't interested in selling anymore. He'd got in with a wealthy crowd in Sydney by then." She pondered a minute. "When I say wealthy, I really mean snobbish."

"Dad says a snob is one who knows the price of everything and the value of nothing."

"David says that? Do you think he really means it?"

It seemed important to her and I was glad that I knew he did.

"Not original, you know. Oscar Wilde said it first, about cynics. But it sums up snobs for me. And your father, eh? Well now, isn't that remarkable. And he was one himself at twenty-one. I'm glad he's grown out of it." She was so busy smiling that I thought she wasn't going to tell me any more, and she didn't.

Because then Roger and Charles came in carrying the beautiful velvet bag that I'd noticed when Charles got off the train. It was a going-away present for me!

"It really is glorious, isn't it?" Roger gloated. "Not new, we mourn, but you just can't buy them nowadays. We don't do so much travelling now, and it just seems right for you, we thought, didn't we, Charles?"

"Roger's idea," smiled Charles. "You don't mind a present that's not brand-new, do you, Kate?"

I could only whisper my delight.

"There, you see, Charles, I told you she'd love it. Much more fitting for a beautiful young lady than that heavy old thing we saw you arrive with." Nothing went unnoticed in Parsons Creek!

My old one *was* heavy. It was real leather though, and Mummy had taken pride in sending me off with it, but it took me only a second to decide that she'd be much happier knowing I wasn't to be burdened down any longer by its tremendous weight. It could so easily give me a permanent curvature of the spine and that would cause her a lot of grief. So I happily accepted the velvet one and offered the old one to Grandma. Then Roger and I tipped all the scraps of material out of their soap box and spent a mad hour squabbling over the packing of them in their new container.

I told them that the priest had talked about the Bellinis at Mass that morning and Roger snorted.

"That's a case of the mills of God grinding slowly, I must say. Aldo's been gone, what is it, almost three years now!"

Grandma tapped him on the head with her thimbled finger.

"Come now, Roger, we've all been rather remiss in looking after the Bellinis, don't you think?"

And Roger, chided, agreed.

24

I now knew exactly how to spend Grandma Dawson's five pounds. As soon as the shops were open on Monday morning I went to see Mr. Eldershaw and explained what I wanted. He didn't want to charge me, but I was determined not to be stuck with that money forever! He was intrigued when I told him what I wanted done next, but bowed to my English eccentricity and summoned Tom from behind the dress materials where he'd been hiding from customers. The two of us went down the stairs to the chilly basement, dry now but still giving off a dank reminder of that flood.

I selected the colors and Tom took off the labels by sliding a thin blade under the paper on each tin. He thought it was a stupid idea and kept telling me so.

"It's much more fun if you don't know the colors," I assured him. "Makes it a marvelous game of surprises. Anyway, how's your girl?"

"Which girl?" I'd caught him out, but he recovered quickly. "Oh, you mean the one I met Saturday night? Oh, she's okay. Really great. Yeah. Name of . . . Sally."

"I'd like to meet her."

"Ah. Yes. Well, you can't. She's gone away. This morning. Had to go . . . to see her sister."

"Oh what a shame, Tom. I'd so like to get to know her."

"Hey! She'll be back next week. You can meet her then. Oh gee, I forgot, you leave tomorrow, don't you. Some other time maybe."

I was tempted to say I'd decided to stay on for another week, just to watch the expression on his face, but I didn't. Leaving Parsons Creek was too serious and sad an occasion to joke about.

When our job was done Tom packed all the tins into a big box and promised to deliver them to Grandma after I had gone back to Sydney. Then he asked me if I'd like to go out with him that evening, but it was my last, and I really wanted to spend it with Gran.

"All right if I come and see you off tomorrow, then?"

I agreed willingly to that.

Working in that basement had given me a terrible thirst, so the only thing to do was to go for a malted milk.

It was just as well I had no intention of making conversation with Roberto, because there were two other female people in the café and they stayed on and on, so that short of ordering a third malted which I couldn't possibly have managed to drink, there was nothing I could do but leave. Roberto was polite. I was very glad to see that business was picking up.

On the way home I passed, of all people, Mrs. Bellini. Out alone in the street for the first time since I'd come to town! She was trotting along with a smile twitching the corner of her mouth, and glancing from side to side as if she were seeing the street for the very first time. We stopped and chatted for a moment.

"I go to help Roberto," she told me. I didn't think he needed any help, but I did feel it was a good idea for his mother to be there with him. She needed the company.

We said good-bye in case I didn't see her again before I left town. She thanked me again for the party, and said people were so kind. Many had come to her at Mass and spoken fondly of her Aldo, and she and Roberto had been invited straight away to lunch. That explained their long absence the day before. I'd gone in during the afternoon to show Mrs. Bellini my new traveling bag and they'd still been out. She went on her way finally, still talking. I called after her.

"Say good-bye to Roberto for me!"

It seemed the best way to take leave of him. Goodness knows I didn't want a farewell scene, specially since we didn't get on at all well.

I went inside and sadly packed my things. The bag was so elegant; the glow from the velvet seemed to enter my fingers when I stroked its glossy surface. I carefully wadded clothing across the bottom and up the sides of it to protect its suede lining from injury from my schoolbooks. I could see that caring for it was going to be a heavy responsibility, but I wouldn't have taken my old leather one back for anything. It was too much to expect that my mother would ever forgive me for exchanging her aristocratic leather for stunning colored velvet, but I'd worry about that when the time came. The velvet was *me*. Both Roger and Charles had assured me that the velvet was me, and I agreed.

Grandma was working at Dr. Browning's house that day, so after lunch I walked up to meet her. I called in at the telephone exchange on the way. Nell Carter was laying waste to another biscuit tin of goodies and offered me the hospitality of the office again.

"Sorry to see you go, dear. It's been a delight having you here, and wasn't that a marvellous party on Saturday? I've been telling folks on the phone here ever since. Patronize the White Rose, I tell them. It's our duty. Part of the war effort. That's what I tell them."

"Maybe you should tell them to patronize the Vesuvio," I suggested. She grinned.

"You're right! Take us a while, I suppose, but they're not a bad lot around here, once you put it to them. By the way, the headmaster's speaking to the school about vandalism. Might do some good with those little hooligans who've been writing on the walls."

From my own experience I knew that the headmaster's speech would certainly go unheard, but I wished him luck. Not that the Bellinis and their problems were any concern of mine anymore.

Grandma was ready to leave when I arrived at Dr. Browning's, so we loaded her basket on the handlebars and I doubled her home. It was late afternoon and cold and Grandma gripped me tightly around the waist and nuzzled her head between my shoulders. I felt warm all through when she did that and the wind brought tears to my eyes.

After dinner she picked up *War and Peace*, then put it down again.

"Time enough to read that when you're not here for company," she said. "But he's not a bad writer, I'll give him that."

Tolstoy had finally made it!

"That reminds me," she went on, "I think I'll give those books back to Charles, make a bit more room

156

in my place, and there's talk of an operation for his cataracts, so he might be wanting to read them himself."

"He doesn't want them back, he told me. Oh, do keep them, Grandma. I like to think of you having them here, words to fill the silence."

"You'll be writing me letters," she answered. "I'll be kept busy reading them, won't I? But I'll have a word with Charles anyway. Now, young Kate. What would you like to talk about?"

"Gnomes."

"Ah yes, the gnomes. Well, your father just didn't want to do anything about them when he came home next time. Didn't want to do anything about anything, really. Just mooned around waiting to get away. Suddenly he hated the place, and everyone in it."

"That was beastly of him."

"No! Bless my soul, girl, he was in love, and suddenly embarrassed by our poverty. He was like his father there, you see. Both of them found it easier to pretend to be rich than to admit to being poor and then do something about it. Your father made up stories of a wealthy, mean old mother to explain his lack of funds. It doesn't matter now anyway. He did what he had to do at the time. You say he's changed and I believe you. People can change."

"I don't think my mother has. Changed. She still needs to be lied to. To be made comfortable, to stop her from being afraid. But he's finished lying about you, Grandma. He just never talks about you."

As soon as I said it I realized that it wasn't the most tactful remark a person could make, but Gran looked pleased.

"That's good. We were close friends once."

"But I know he thinks about you, because he's always telling me to be still and think."

We talked for a long time. It was a cozy conversation, heads close and feet lined up together inside the open oven. I know it wasn't necessary to hold my face so close to Grandma's when I was speaking to her, she could read my lips quite well right across the room. But my feet were cold.

At about midnight we came back to the gnomes. They'd been niggling at my mind and it was worse than I had thought. Dad had even borrowed money from the bank and the manager had harassed Grandma to pay it back.

"The one gnome David did try to sell he took to the bank manager and the rotter pretended he'd brought it as a gift and kept it. That's why Charles played that trick on him. Jaunting Jack. Did it to cheer me up, bless him. It did, too. Made me feel quite cheery as I went in to make the repayments, knowing what Jack was up to. Oh, your father paid the money back," she hurried to explain as she watched my face subsiding into gloom. "When he graduated and got a job he sent a letter telling me he was going to marry your mother, and there was a check inside."

I was glad he'd paid back the money—if he had. Grandma might be telling me that just to be kind. It certainly was a bleak way to treat one's mother. I would look more closely at my father when I saw him again, I decided.

"Yes," she went on. "It's still out there, buried under the gnomes. When the letter came and I knew he'd not be coming back I used the last of the cement to plant those gnomes and I shoveled the check in under their feet. I was angry and I hated them at the time, but over the years I've grown used to having the little fellows out there. They could do with a coat of paint, though."

"I'll paint them for you when I come back. At Christmas."

"Coming back, then, are you?"

She seemed quite pleased.

25

My train left at a quarter to one. Grandma had to go to work and we'd said good-bye the night before, so I wheeled her bicycle to the gate for her and she gave me a quick hug as she left. Tom was coming to fetch me to the train at twelve. I suppose lunch hours were elastic for him, since his grandpa owned the store.

Mrs. Bellini came in, weeping *fortissimo*, and gave me a magnificent box of chocolates which I packed on top of my velvet case to give to Grandma Dawson, guilty at not having thought to buy something sooner.

That gave me the idea to get something for Grandpa Dawson as well, so I popped down to the Vesuvio to see if there was something there he might like.

Again Roberto was not alone. This time it was Helen, Jim's girl, perched on one of the stools, languidly scooping minute portions of ice cream out of a long glass parfait dish.

I talked to her for a while. Roberto leaned against the other side of the counter and watched the street outside, then I ordered malted milk for old times' sake. Still she scooped and licked at her tiny blobs of ice cream. I'd miss my train if the stupid idiot didn't hurry up. By yoyoing the level of my straw I managed to prolong my drink and we went over *Pimpernel Smith* in detail, then *The Smiling Ghost*, and many other pictures she had seen. Useless to include Roberto in the conversation as he only saw the inside of the theater during the intermission, while he sold his tray of confectionery, but Helen tried! Then she talked of their school days when they were apparently *terribly* good friends and had done all sorts of *terribly* amusing things together. I was bored silly and completely fed up. I'd arrived at the end of my glass in spite of my delays. I'd have to go.

Then Roberto spoke. "We weren't such good friends, Helen."

Helen smirked. "Maybe we weren't. Have to do something about that, won't we?"

"You want another sundae?"

"Not just yet, thanks. Haven't finished this one yet."

"Just saw your boss go past in his car, must have come back for something."

She was off the stool in a second and out the door. I waved a cheerful good-bye to her, then turned back to Roberto. He was smiling! Ever so faintly, but smiling. I hadn't realized how white his teeth were.

"You want another malted?" he asked.

"Oh yes please," I heard myself answer.

"No, you don't," he said, "you drink too many of those things and you'll end up with bad skin."

He'd known me four weeks and he hadn't noticed that I already *had* bad skin!

But in case I became too elated he then said, "You're leaving today." Not "Sorry you're leaving today," not "I wish you weren't leaving today," just "You're leaving today."

"Look," I said as I stood up to go, "I'm sorry we

161

seem to have started off on the wrong foot, but there's no reason why we can't be civil to each other, is there? I'm coming back for Christmas and it upsets Grandma if I don't get on with her neighbors."

He looked me right in the eye and smiled again. He knew Grandma too! I felt the blush surge around my ears and up my forehead.

"I can be civil to you, Katharine," he said quietly. "And I'm grateful for what you did for us. Thank you."

There are times when I suspect that I may be suffering from a form of split personality. I distinctly hear my voice saying words that I swear I've never thought, and that I know I would never have uttered if I had. It's a very disconcerting affliction, particularly for a person of my age who spends most of her waking hours trying to avoid being noticed by those around her.

"But you don't really like me, do you?" this voice said.

He stared out of the door for a long time, then looked back at me and gently answered, "No."

It came to me that I'd been meeting far too many honest people lately. "May I inquire what it is about me that you don't like?" The voice pressed on while I peered intently down into my glass in case I'd missed something. Sometimes the malted-milk powder makes a little cake down the bottom there.

"Well, that's one of the things"—chattily, as if we were just making conversations, for goodness' sake. " 'May I inquire,' 'spiffy.' And so on."

"I'm sorry if the way I talk . . ."

"It's not the way you talk. That's okay, sounds good. It's the things you say. Everything's 'ghastly,' and that '*mirabile dictu*,' and making up those stories about your father . . ."

This from a person who used to pretend his name

was Bert Bell! I would not cry in front of this boorish boy, so I collected my handbag from the counter and turned away.

And three stupid people chose that very moment to dash in off the street and plonk their ghastly selves down at one of the tables.

But *mirab*— Oh joy! Roberto just took no notice of them at all, he came right around from behind the counter and caught up with me as I arrived at the doorway, and he took my hand and sort of shook it and said, "Good-bye, Katharine, I'll see you at Christmastime. Maybe we'll get to know each other better then."

Maybe we would. I didn't know. Didn't know if I could change enough to suit him, and didn't know if I really wanted to. I shook his hand in return. It was very large and warm.

"Good-bye, Roberto," I said.

One of the men at the table shouted, "Hey! We gonna get any service here?"

So I turned away and focused my eyes carefully on the cracks in the footpath as I walked along to Park Street and Grandma's house. I'd forgotten to buy something for Grandpa, but he wouldn't mind sharing the chocolates.

I said good-bye to the bees and the gnomes before Tom arrived. With him came Charles and Roger for a final farewell, then the two of us set out, Tom carrying the velvet bag and me the big soap box filled with honey, bacon, butter and cream for the Dawsons. Around the corner by the bank we went, past Eldershaw's Emporium and a beaming Mr. Eldershaw, slowly toward the Vesuvio. I racked my brain for something bright and snappy to be saying to Tom as we passed, without result, and I also decided I wouldn't look inside.

When I looked inside I saw the back of Roberto's

head as he took a box of sweets from the shelf behind the counter. I was very pleased that he had yet another customer.

We arrived at the station, and I turned for a last look at the little town. A few cars were parked along the street, and not many people were about. Parsons Creek looked just as it had on the day I arrived. I turned and followed Tom through the gate onto the platform.

We sat on one of the long wooden seats while Tom copied out the Dawsons' address and telephone number for when he came down to Sydney to enlist.

"They'll take me all right, and as a pilot too. Too right they will."

I hoped they would if that was what he wanted, and we held relaxed and friendly hands until the train came in. Mr. McCann, pigeon expert and Grandma's foe, came forward and opened the door of the compartment, then tipped his cap and went back to chat with the guard at the back of the train, where the porter was busy with his trolley. Tom jumped inside and put my bag and the box on the rack above my seat. Then he came down again. He shuffled a bit and said, "Good-bye, Kate, gee it's been great knowing you." Then he grabbed me in a great hug and kissed me. I breathed desperately through my nose, reminded of being at the dentist, and just before I expired he let me go. "See you in Sydney, then."

"Thank you for seeing me off, good luck with the Air Force." Then I climbed aboard and we were moving.

Tom ran along beside the carriage until the fence at the end of the platform stopped him. I watched Parsons Creek slide away, first the bitumen streets, then the unmade roads, the smaller houses, then the vast storage shed where Grandma and I had skated.

And there she was! A tiny figure in the center of the big shed. Wearing her best tablecloth and sweater, with the dear stripey beanie on her head, waving a large tea towel. She must have pedaled like mad from her job that day to be at the shed in time.

I flung down the window and knelt on the seat and waved and shouted and bellowed and screeched like a howling dervish, knowing she couldn't hear a word of it, and not caring a bit. Then the huge concrete bulk of the silo abruptly cut off our farewells. I closed the window and sat down and opened the parcel of sandwiches she had prepared for me. The honey tasted salty from my tears, but I ate them all, then I crunched the noisy, perfumed apple from Mrs. North's orchard, until all that was left were a tiny bit of stalk and six pips. I slipped them into the side pocket of my handbag to plant back in Sydney, or maybe at home in England. I would be coming back at Christmastime to Parsons Creek. I wanted to help Grandma rob the bees and finish the patchwork quilt, paint the house and restore the gnomes, and perhaps I'd persuade Roberto to hang Vesuvio on the wall of his café again.

I felt more cheerful then, so I looked around at the other passengers in my compartment and gave them a smile. Didn't bother to conserve my lips this time. I've got fat lips, but that's the way I am.

MAUREEN POPLE grew up during World War II in country towns in New South Wales, Australia. She has won numerous awards for her stories, plays, and television scripts, including the National Short Story of the Year Award and the Henry Lawson Award for Prose, and recently published her second novel for young adults, *A Nugget of Gold*. She is married, with two grown daughters, and lives in Sydney.

DEBORAH HAUTZIG...

"is indeed an author to watch!"
—*School Library Journal* (starred review)

HEY, DOLLFACE

Fifteen-year-old Val Hoffman's dreary prospects for a lonely year at the stuffy Garfield School for Girls are brightened when she meets Chloe Fox, whose irreverent sense of the outrageous is the perfect antidote. Before long, Val and Chloe are spending all their time together, sharing the special secrets that only best friends have. The closeness of their friendship takes on new meaning, though, when Val becomes confused by the growing strength of her feelings for Chloe. What if this is more than friendship? And what happens if Chloe feels the same way?

"One of the best young adult novels available."
—Norma Klein, *Ms.*

SECOND STAR TO THE RIGHT

Should a few extra pounds matter to Leslie Hiller, a bright, talented, attractive teenager who leads a privileged life in New York City? Unfortunately, they do. Because, despite all her accomplishments, Leslie is driven by her desire for perfection in all things. And to her, being thin is being perfect. Although she starts her diet thinking that all she needs is a little more discipline, things go horribly awry when her self-control turns into self-destruction. Like it or not, she must face up to the fact that she's starving herself—to death.

"The best book yet on anorexia nervosa."
—*School Library Journal* (starred review)
An American Book Award nominee

BORZOI SPRINTERS PUBLISHED BY ALFRED A. KNOPF, INC.

PHILIP PULLMAN...

"is a master of atmosphere and style."
—*School Library Journal*

THE RUBY IN THE SMOKE

"Beware the seven blessings...." When sixteen-year-old Sally Lockhart utters these words, an employee of her late father dies of fear. Thus begins her terrifying journey into the seamy underworld of Victorian London in search of clues that will solve the puzzle of her father's death. Pursued by villains and cutthroats at every turn, she at last uncovers two dark mysteries. Sally soon learns that she is the key to both—and that it's worth her very life to find out why.

Winner of the International Reading Association's
Children's Book Award
An ALA Best Book for Young Adults

SHADOW IN THE NORTH

It's six years later, and Sally is now a financial consultant in London. When one of her clients loses a fortune on the strength of her advice, she's determined to recover the money. Soon Sally, her paramour Frederick, and their friend Jim are hot on the trail of Axel Bellmann, a wealthy, unscrupulous businessman. What they uncover is a plot so diabolical that it could eventually subvert the entire civilized world—and if Bellmann has his way, Sally and her friends won't even live long enough to see it happen!

An ALA Best Book for Young Adults
A *Booklist* Editors' Choice
Nominated for the Edgar Allan Poe Award for Best Mystery

BORZOI SPRINTERS PUBLISHED BY ALFRED A. KNOPF, INC.

Introducing the
ALANNA
series by Tamora Pierce:

"Marvelously satisfying!"
—*School Library Journal*

ALANNA: THE FIRST ADVENTURE

Alanna of Trebond has always yearned to become a warrior maiden, and she's not about to let a little thing like the wrong gender or her mysterious, magical power known as the "Gift" get in the way. Disguised as a boy, she gains admittance to the palace military academy and quickly establishes herself as the most talented of the new knights-in-training. But maintaining the secrets of her womanhood and her healing magic becomes more and more difficult over time. And when only sorcery can save the prince from a fatal illness, Alanna faces the most difficult decision of her life. Should she use her Gift, thus revealing her true nature? Or lose her dearest friend for the sake of her most cherished dream?

"A lively, fascinating tale."—*Booklist*
"Smooth and spirited!"
—*Bulletin of the Center for Children's Books*

IN THE HAND OF THE GODDESS

Alanna, now Prince Jonathan's official squire, has sworn to protect him from harm. It takes all of her considerable skills to unmask the mysterious, evil sorcerer who is intent on destroying her prince. And when she does, no one is more terrified than Alanna, who finds herself face to face with none other than the prince's own cousin, Duke Roger—the most powerful sorcerer in the land!

"Alanna is a charming heroine!"—*School Library Journal*
"An action-filled adventure novel. Recommended."
—*Fantasy Review*

BORZOI SPRINTERS PUBLISHED BY ALFRED A. KNOPF, INC.